Cream of Asbestos Soup, Please

Ninety Years of Martini Stories

Gerrie Martini

outskirts press

Cream of Asbestos Soup, Please
Ninety Years of Martini Stories

v2.0

Outskirts Press, Inc.
http://www.outskirtspress.com

Paperback ISBN: 978-1-9772-4558-8

PRINTED IN THE UNITED STATES OF AMERICA

This book is dedicated to my five delightful amazing children Marie, Bob, Betty, Patty and Joan and my twelve marvelous grandchildren who are absolutely perfect in every way! and my fifteen great-grandchildren who are enchanting and also— perfect in every way!

PREFACE

I have searched my brain and mind in order to remember stories that I've enjoyed throughout my life. The older I get the more there is to remember and the more I forget.

There are many times when I forgot what I remembered!

Sometimes I thought of a story while falling asleep in bed, and the next day I could not remember one thing about it. I began to write notes during the night. I have had fun remembering and writing stories from experiences that have happened in my lifetime.

As I write, I try to remember a word that will describe exactly what I want to say, but I just cannot find it. Sometimes it will pop into my head and I have to write it down immediately lest I forget it once again and lose it forever. It's the same with stories; my mind plays tricks on me. I imagine searching through billions of brain cells just to find and remember one story or word. It's got to be in there somewhere, but the trick is to track it down and find the location.

During the time I have written this book, I have developed a renewed appreciation and admiration for authors. I can't imagine working this hard year after year for a lifetime, the way most authors do.

I have spent an enormous amount of time

researching and rewriting each and every page until I was satisfied with the result. In creating this book, the characters have become like family to me, and I know them body and soul.

I started this work at the age of ninety. I must have been crazy, but I've enjoyed every step of the way. As a result, I have had to sacrifice much of the reading I would normally do. I'm looking forward to reclaiming, at last, the time that reading a book requires. During the years that I was raising my five wonderful children, the only reading time available was filled with the stories we read to our children.

The stories in this book are all based on real experiences embellished from time to time with the work of my imagination. All the medical stories and all the school stories are real life experiences of my family or friends. I have tried to equip my characters with humor and weave the stories into their lives as I imagined them to be.

My close companions in this endeavor have been my dictionary, my thesaurus, and my trusty typewriter. I do not do computers. I don't have the mindset for them. I am what I am!

I am so proud of my family. I have five amazing children who have lived their lives having astonishing families and careers. I have twelve extraordinary grandchildren, and fifteen great-grandchildren, all of them wonderful.

I grew up in Stevens Point, and lived in Wausaukee, Goodman Ranger Station, Rhinelander, Madison and now La Crosse, and I have met so many great people in all of these places. I have loved every one of these Wisconsin towns. Each and every one was an adventure.

I lived in four different apartments in my twelve years in Madison, and my family moved me from place to place every time in just one weekend. My sister-in-law scolded me and said I would drive them nuts.

Life is an adventure.

PROLOGUE

The story in the book starts in Italy in the city of Palermo in Sicily. There is a devastating mystery in the Martini family that has caused the family to get on a boat and go to America, acting with great speed. More on the voyage later, and on to their destination, Madison, Wisconsin.

This book takes place in Madison, the capitol of Wisconsin. Madison is a city of liberal, nonconventional people who believe in the essential goodness of humankind and individual freedom. Many people in Madison are delightfully quirky and whimsical, and the parades and festivals are fabulous. Everyone has fun in Madison.

The city is an isthmus of land connecting two bodies of water, Lake Monona and Lake Mendota. The two lakes are beautiful, and there are always sailboats and fishing boats on the water. The UW Union building is right on Lake Mendota and the students and townspeople love to spend time there.

Every Fourth of July the UW Union is filled with people of all ages, who celebrate with food and drink. There are live bands and people have fun watching people and playing games at the colorful, iconic tables and chairs all over the sprawling patio.

Some read, others knit.

As the darkness comes, a gigantic firework display with synchronized classical music is watched and heard with awe. Many people take their boats to the Union to watch this sensational program, and the lake is alive with lighted boats. It is the best Fourth of July program in America! The lights on the boats look like sparkling fireflies in the dark.

During the summer months, the Capitol Square has many activities. The one I like best is Concerts on the Square, which is held for six Wednesdays in a row in the summer. There are thousands who come and sit in camping chairs or sit on blankets and eat the fabulous food from the food carts that offer food from all over the world. the ice cream is so good, and there are so many interesting flavors that it's hard to decide which one to order. There is a solid mass of people on chairs or blankets on all four sides of the Capitol Square.

The Madison Concert Band plays extraordinary classical music and we are all spellbound. This is a concert for people of all ages, and there are families with babies, small children dancing to the music, and old people with wide straw hats. There is every kind of clothing and it's fun to people-watch while you listen to the music. Some have very elegant gowns, and some are flashy or gaudy.

Another favorite of mine is the Farmer's Market at the Capitol Square. Every Saturday in the spring, summer and fall there are booths all around the square, with incredible produce, flowers, meat, honey and plants. There are also a variety of baked goods that are so delicious: donuts, cookies, sweet rolls, breads, etc. Street musicians are everywhere.

Raging Grannies sing on a corner, and political

groups have tables. Madison has a reputation for having versatile festivals all over the city. Just to name a few: German Fest, Italian Fest, Native American Fest, Irish Fest, Polish Fest, Swedish Fest, French Fest, Thai Fest, and many music festivals. All of these festivals share ethnic food, dancing, costumes, music and drinks. Everyone has a good time at the festivals.

Jazz at Five is fun at the Capitol Square with many music groups performing.

Again, there are food carts and street musicians. Once a year there is Opera in the Park free of charge for anyone who wants to go. Everyone brings their food, or they can buy food there. One has to bring their own chairs or blankets and thousands come early to visit with friends or read in this beautiful park. This is opera under starry skies.

Wisconsin people love folk music and polka bands and dancing. There are festivals for these as well in Madison. Little kids dance with their parents and grandparents and people of all ages love these dances.

The beautiful Wisconsin Capitol building is 580,000 square feet in size and is 284 feet tall, the tallest building in Madison. No building in Madison can be built taller than the Capitol. The dome has a statue of Wisconsin, which many people misidentify as Lady, or Miss Forward. This statue has been standing atop the dome since 1914.The dome itself is made of 8,909,200 pounds of cast iron bolted together in a masterpiece of American will and ingenuity.

The inside of the Capitol has marble floors and stairways with wonderful mosaics and sculptures. The Capitol houses both chambers of the Wisconsin legislature along with the Wisconsin Supreme Court and the

Office of the Governor.

A Wisconsin Christmas tree is brought in every year, and it is adorned with charming, delightful ornaments that school children from all over the state have made, along with thousands of lights. It is a stunning tree.

Madison people all love the Henry Vilas Zoo, which is free of charge. The 5-Star Zoo is 28 acres of exotic animals and reptiles, with a train and carousel to delight little kids. Families have birthday parties there, and there are summer school programs there as well.

The 5-Star Olbrick Botanical Gardens is 16 acres of flowers, trees, shrubs, sculptures, grasses, and a bridge to the Thai House. This marvelous building was sent from the Thai government in appreciation for the Thai students that came to UW in Madison. It was sent in many pieces and put together here by Thai workers, and is a favorite place for Madison people, with the lovely pool near by. The Butterfly Exhibit is held in the fall every year with many butterfly species.

The University of Wisconsin is a public research university founded in 1848 when Wisconsin achieved statehood and is the flagship campus of the University of Wisconsin system. It is a prolific research institution with students, staff and faculty members partaking in a world-class education, and solving real world problems . UW research has $1.2 billion per year and has been awarded 41 Pulitzer Prizes. UW discovered vitamins in the 1910's, cultivated embryonic stem cells in the 1990's, and helped unearth a human species in the 2010's.

There are 43,820 students at the UW in Madison and about 5,000 international students from 130 countries around the world. UW is among the largest of international students in the country, with 400-degree tracts.

Parts of the Statue of Liberty appear in Lake Mendota in February on the frozen lake. The head, arm and torch appear at the Union for the annual Winter Carnival.

Along with pink flamingoes on the formal grounds of Bascom Hall and the Statue of Liberty in front of the Union, there are many other exotic, amusing, funny events that happen at the UW.

Frank Lloyd Wright originally proposed a design for a "dream civic center" in 1938. His architectural vision for the city of Madison —a curvilinear gathering place— finally was built in 1997. Built on the shore of Lake Monona, Monona Terrace is an amazing community and convention center, which is used for huge gatherings and also smaller gatherings and is located in the heart of downtown Madison.

Another amazing building very close to the state Capitol is the 5-Star Overture Center for the Arts. It houses the performing arts center and the Madison Museum of Contemporary Art and many smaller theaters. The Overture is a stunning architectural landmark in the heart of Madison's thriving cultural arts district. Broadway plays and musicals and the Madison Symphony Orchestra perform there, as well as operas, children's plays, and the Madison Ballet.

Bucky Badger is the mascot for the UW, and there are many photos, statues, and souvenirs available during athletic games. The Badger football games are so much fun with the sensational UW band and loads of razzmatazz. The fifth quarter music and frolicking is really quite extraordinary.

Many of the other Badger sports are equally fun and popular with basketball for women and men playing at the spectacular Kohl Center. Men and women's hockey teams also play at the Kohl Center as well as concerts and other entertainment for large groups of people. Water sports tennis, baseball and many other sports are offered here as well.

Madison has a reputation for having a variety of good restaurants. Campus restaurants are popular with Dotty Dumplings, Dowry and the Nitty Gritty (where you get a free beer on your birthday). In addition, there are Mexican, Italian, Japanese, Chinese, Irish, gyros, steakhouses, seafood, oyster bars, and sandwich places, and some of them are very elegant.

Madison also has top-notch schools from pre-K to university doctorate.

Madison parks and pools are splendid and all over the city. There are active senior centers and a variety of churches. It seems like Madison has it all!

OUR STORYTELLERS

Tony and Francesca Martini were born in Palermo, Italy, and immigrated to America. Sam is the grandson of Tony and Francesca.

Rosita is Sam's wife.

Gino is the son of Sam and Rosita. Carmen is Gino's wife.

Michael is the son of Gino and Carmen. Olive is the daughter of Gino and Carmen.

Bubbles (Alayna) is the daughter of Gino and Carmen. Sherry is the daughter of Gino and Carmen.

Ginny is the daughter of Gino and Carmen. Eric Schwantes marries Ginny.

Sean Schwantes is Eric's father. Lydia is Sean's wife.

Nick Schwantes is Sean and Lydia's daughter.

Margo Schwantes is Sean and Lydia's daughter.

	Martini Family				
Tony	**married**	Francesca			
	children				
August	Sam	5 children left in Italy			
married	married				
Angelina	Rosita				
	Children				
	Gino	(& 5 other children)			
	married		Schwantes Family		
	Carmen				
			Sean	married	Lydia
	children			**children**	
	Ginny	married	Eric	Nick	Margo
	Bubbles				
	Michael				
	Olive				
	Sherry				

MAFIA BEGINNINGS

Early in the history of Italy, the country was organized along the lines of city states that had their own officials, laws, organizational structures, police militias and their own means of enforcement. Sicily would likely have been organized along these lines. In the latter half of the nineteenth century these structures began to loosen, as people began to assert their right to become involved in the way they were governed.

The city states began to lose their previous absolute control over the way thingshad always been done. And I believe that, as part of the ongoing transition, *what was allowed crossed paths with what you could get away with*. And that may be the way in which organized crime began.

In the absence of sufficient state-mandated law enforcement, powerful individuals also began taking on the role of enforcers. You could say they did not hesitate to work both sides of the street, and *enforcement always came at a price*. By the 1870's the mafia beginnings were recognizably there.

TONY'S STORY

Allow me to introduce myself. I'm Tony Martini, proud to call Italy, more specifically the city of Palermo on the island of Sicily, as the land of my birth, Palermo is a city on the northern coast of Sicily. It is a city at once ancient and modern, known for centuries for its enormous semicircular harbor, well-protected, with waters deep enough to accommodate any ship sailing the high seas.

Given its location and desirability, generations have fought over it, going back to the Phoenicians, Greeks, Romans, barbarian tribes and others up to the recent past.

So that, while technically Italian, I've inherited bits and pieces from all these different societies as they came through. Remarkable, when you think about it.

I was born into a traditional Italian family in Palermo, never thinking that I would live in any other place. Things, however, do not always go the way you assumed they would. There is a saying that you should always expect the unexpected. What on earth would the unexpected have to offer in Palermo? Well, let me tell you about that.

I became involved, with a small group of people, in a crime that should have been relatively straightforward and risk-free. Unfortunately, it didn't go that way, and what started out as a simple robbery ended up in a brutal murder. I was not responsible for the murder, but I was willing to take the blame for my family. It seemed the best way forward, and if I could leave Palermo immediately, my safety would not be in question.

I did, however, have my wife, Francesca, and our children. Francesca may be small in stature, but she can be a formidable opponent. This was not going to go down easily with her or with any of the rest of them. I gave them only enough of the truth to make the necessity of leaving immediately apparent and believable, even if mostly unexplained. To guarantee our safety, a large part of what happened had to be omitted.

I bought time by telling Francesca that I would explain it all the next day when we were aboard ship bound for America and would have more time to talk. This was a lie, as the truth had to stay locked up with me for the rest of my life.

From that time on, our marriage was never really the same; the need for secrecy would become an enduring wall between the two of us that neither of us could ever bridge. Francesca was sure I had something to hide, and she was right. She also believed that I kept the truth to myself because I didn't trust her. I didn't trust *anyone,* not even the person who had been closest to me. In many respects, from that day forward, though seemingly together as a couple, we lived in separate worlds and went our separate ways.

The truth is, the burglary was a simple thing that we had done many times. It was wrong, we knew, but the business we stole from was crooked and took advantage of poor people. We tried to justify our exploits as sort of Robin Hood theory.

But when the murder took place, we knew we were in trouble because the family was vicious and held a grudge against anyone who crossed them. The family had seven sons and many uncles, and they would get their revenge one way or the other.

They were ruthless. This was the beginning of the Italian Mafia, and our family was scared and worried.

Our family decided that one of us would have to take the blame, and we all knew all of our lives would be at stake if one of us did not. I decided that I was the one because I was the oldest brother. I insisted that the family pay all the expenses to cover our trip to America. We had to act fast and not tell anyone our plans.

We had a family meeting with our parents present, and they said they would move into our house and take care of the children. We are so sad that our children insisted that they stay in Palermo, and we didn't have time to talk them into coming with us.. All of us are stubborn and ornery and we could not talk them into it. August, his wife Angelina and their children Samuel, Reiny and Marcella were the only ones who would come with us, the other five refused. They were old enough to make their own decisions, but their refusal came as a shock. It very likely meant that we would never see them again.

I am so sad for all of us. Why did we do the burglary? I swear to God that I will never ever break the law again, and I will live a good and productive life in America. My parents are concerned and horrified about the whole thing. They, too, know the family and they know how dangerous they are.

My parents and Francesca's parents and the two families will be criticized and attacked but I hope in time things will get better. I hate to put them through all this— especially the children. I love my family and Francesca's family. Francesca will never forgive me.

For the next twenty-four hours things moved very quickly. We had to organize, pack what little we could take, and present ourselves at the ship at first light the next morning. We would travel in steerage, and the voyage would take twenty-one days.

We also had to change our last name to Martini, and Francesca did not take kindly to that. I took care of everything that we would need; first light did, indeed, see us on the pier waiting to board.

Preparing for twenty-one days at sea is no easy task. Bringing food that would not spoil was a priority. We had two trunks to pack, and that's where the food went: oranges, lemons, rice, pasta, raisins, dates, figs, other dried fruit; sardines, dried fish, hard candy, dried vegetables, apples, carrots, potatoes, rutabagas, cheese, oats, salt, garlic, onions, honey, crackers, jams and jellies. I also bought a large cooking pot and four pails that would nest together and fit in one of the trunks.

The other priority was the cost of our passage—$10,00 a person. In normal circumstances, this would have been 'way beyond our means, and Francesca knew it. I managed to find enough to pay our way. How I did it was part of the secret that could not be shared. Good wife that she was, resentments and all, she dutifully followed along, and at first light we stood ready and waiting to mount the gang-plank as the ship prepared to get underway. As far as I could tell, there was no system of reserving passage. You simply showed up at the pier, paid your fare, grabbed your luggage and boarded.

As we board the ship, we go down, down, down, into the bottom of the ship.

Everything looks and feels dark and gloomy. Steerage passage is not the way you want to travel if you have a choice. It's the lowest part of the boat, and there are few, if any, amenities. Sanitation is minimal and the space is extremely crowded. Water and fresh air are priorities; with any luck we would get enough of both to make it through to our destination. It took a lot of time for the ship's crews to load sufficient coal, water and all of the other provisions needed for crossing the Atlantic Ocean.

We went from Palermo to Salerno the first day, and we picked up more passengers and cargo. We continued on to Naples the second day and picked up more passengers and cargo. Then on to Genoa and to Marseilles and to Barcelona, and we were all seasick because of the high winds. Good thing we have a lot of pails with us!

If you are on land, the pavement under your feet is stable. Whether you are walking, running, sitting or sleeping, the earth doesn't move beneath you. A ship, however, is a different matter. The minute it begins to move through the water, the stability of being on land ceases.

Even the most stable vessel is subject to pitch and roll as it moves forward.

Variations such as these may be scarcely noticed

or, in heavy seas, they can be dramatic indeed. The body's balance mechanism is attuned to motion on land. Once the ship is underway, this mechanism is immediately occupied with trying to establish and maintain balance in new circumstances. The immediate result is seasickness, which can be violent in nature and totally disabling. There is little to be done except to wait it out. They tell us that it takes several days to "get your sea-legs". I believe it.

We were all curious about our trip, and couldn't imagine that we were going to all these places. We had spent our entire lives in Palermo. Our next stop was Valencia and by then we had our appetites back and we felt pretty good. We all thanked God for that. We had more than enough food and were able to share with others, especially the children, who didn't have enough. Minus the time spent coping with seasickness, we had many more days to go.

Now we could not see land and we settled into our routine of meals, games, including chess, trying to keep clean and getting along with the 1500 people in steerage. Every day we gathered to begin our study of English, using the books I had bought along.

We were allowed up on deck for one hour a day. The children were told that under no circumstances could they misbehave. If they did, we would lose our fresh air privileges. That was enough to convince them to be on their best behavior. Getting fresh sea air was the best part of the day.

The next best thing for us was at night when fellow travelers would tell stories about their families, and after that we sang songs in Italian. Several of us had musical instruments to play, and that was fun for all.

After that we all prayed and gave thanks for a safe day on the ocean.

At long last, we saw the memorable and breath-taking sight of the Statue of Liberty, and we all gave thanks to God for getting us here safe and sound. We packed our things and got ready to get off the boat. We were very nervous about passing the tests at Ellis Island, as we had heard that we had to be healthy and happy to pass. We worried that we could be sent back to Italy if we didn't pass.

We then gave our names, which were added to the passenger manifest. As we left the ship, our names were checked off the same manifest. That's all there was to it. What we had in our favor when we presented ourselves for examination were cheerful faces, clean clothing and a positive attitude. This did the trick, and we passed with flying colors.

We breathed a sigh of relief and made our way ashore. It was good to be on land again. Our immediate need was a good meal and a bed for the night. Tomorrow we would begin the plan for the rest of our journey, since we had almost another thousand miles to go before we would finally arrive at Madison and the Greenbush and a new place we would eventually call home. I loaded up on food to take on the train, and then bought seven tickets for the train ride, for our family of seven.

The train ride was interesting going through the states to get to Wisconsin. I hoped my relatives would meet us at the train in Madison. This country is so huge! We saw so many farms, cities, etc. I hope and pray that everyone will like America, and that it will work out for us. I have to put up a brave front for my family. I am sad to say that Francesca cried a lot on the way to America. What have I done?

I was relieved that my uncle did meet us at the train station. He seemed excited about having us live with his family. They live in Greenbush, a neighborhood in Madison where many immigrants have settled. It looks so prosperous and clean. I think we will like it here.

Now we all work hard to learn English, and I have a job in a hardware store. I am amazed, and so happy to have this job. I will work very hard.

As the years go by, we go through the Great Depression, but we have work and food to eat. Thank God for the Pelliteris. The hardware store is the center of my life. My boss has taught me how to run the store, and so much more. We have a circle of friends who come every day to play chess or card games and have coffee. It's almost like Italy! When Louie, the owner of the store retired, I happily bought the store, which was my dream. I love the store and now it is mine.

Francesca remains cool to me and I don't think she will ever forgive me. She still does not know the whole story of why we had to leave Palermo, and I cannot tell her.

She agonizes when we get pictures and letters from family in Italy. I am very sad about that, too.

I have not told Francesca that I received a letter from my father telling me that our oldest son, Vito was killed in Palermo under very mysterious circumstances right after we left Palermo. Vito was found near the ocean. There was a note pinned on his clothing saying, "An eye for an eye and a tooth for a tooth."

I hope that Francesca will never find out about this. It would kill her!

I wrote to my father and told him that the family should not retaliate by killing another member of the Mafia family. That could go on and on with many killings. I hope he can convince the rest of our hotheaded family.

THE GREENBUSH

The Greenbush is a neighborhood in Madison, Wisconsin that began to take shape around 1900. It was often referred to as Madison's Ellis Island, as many immigrants, new to American shores, gravitated to it and settled there. Among those settlers was a growing contingent of Italians, many of them from Sicily.

The "Bush", as it was informally known, was comprised of a 10-block area bordered by Park and Regent streets and West Washington Avenue. Within these bounds could be found the glories of the old-world culture flourishing within the confines of the new. The Bush was a big triangle of fifty-two acres, a melting pot of vibrant cultures that sometimes blended into wonderful harmony and sometimes clashed in tragic ways.

By 1870, 25,000 Italians had arrived in America. Between 1880 and 1924 more than 4,000,000 people arrived on our shores, half of these between 1900 and 1910.

After WWI enormous numbers of people were on the move, most driven by economic hardship. They weren't just coming from Italy. They were coming from all over Europe, including the British Isles.

In 1900, fifteen people had settled in the Bush. In 1910 there were 446; in 1916 there were 1100. At that time, thirty percent of the Greenbush population was under the age of thirty. There were thirty single males to every single female. The inhabitants were mostly poor and were not exactly welcome elsewhere in Madison. Men came ahead in hopes of earning enough money so the rest of the family could follow, and in time they did.

In Catherine Tripalin Murray's *Grandmothers of Greenbush* we find the following words, "When we return to the memory of our grandmothers, we see dusty upstairs attics where things were stored in old trunks and boxes, and basements where bread was baked on hot summer days and served in the coolness of its depths at suppertime. We feel intricate needlework that covered dining room tables, beds and davenport arms; end tables where vases, statues and pictures of loved ones rested.

"We remember bed linens draped from second floor windows to air in the crispness of the early morning and smell the fragrance of hand-scrubbed floors covered with newspapers to protect them until company arrived. We savor memories of kitchens where kettles filled with soups and sauces were stirred with long-handled wooden spoons and ovens warm to the touch with nourishment for the family and anyone else who happened to stop by at the last moment.

"We think of freshly squeezed lemonade to pack in picnic baskets carried to nearby parks, rolling pins that created flaky-crusted pies to cool on window sills, and balmy evenings when friends and neighbors gathered on front porches and talked until it was time to climb the stairs to bedrooms where seeds were planted for new generations.

"African-American and Italian boys played sports together on an abandoned lot off Regent Street; the

Jewish proprietor of Movick's grocery store encouraged my great-grandmother to buy food for her family on credit when her husband had missed work due to illness, and very few people locked their doors." Of such things was this community within a community called the Greenbush made.

Madison's first neighborhood center, Neighborhood House, was established in 1916, and Columbus Park, now Brittingham Park, was the site of frequent neighborhood picnics on warm summer afternoons. Neighborhood House still thrives, albeit not in the original building on Mills, near Regent.

At the time of its founding, Neighborhood House was the centerpiece of efforts to help new immigrants adjust to their new exciting lives as Americans, Neighbors gathered to sew, cook, learn American recipes, improve their English and work toward attaining their goal of citizenship.

The Greenbush Neighborhood was also an early template for today's urban gardens movement. Virtually everyone in the Bush had a garden, and when the tomatoes ripened, wonderful things happened.

Catherine Murray says, "And in the heat of summer's August, when the tomatoes turned a brilliant red all the Italian women in the Bush would get their tomato boards out of storage in preparation for the making of tomato pastes...and soon the entire neighborhood was fragrant with the aroma of tomatoes, and part of their culture was being preserved." And it didn't stop with tomatoes. Italian immigrants waited for grapes to arrive on the Milwaukee Road trains so they could be turned into homemade wine.

Unfortunately, the reality of life in Greenbush as

experienced by the people who actually lived there was tarnished by perceptions from outside. Woodridge reports that while children of different heritages played well together inside the Bush they were often taunted when they left the neighborhood together. Even a modern-day historian continually refers to the old Bush as being "a festering slum."

It is due to this lack of understanding of a complex, imperfect, yet functioning neighborhood by those in power, that the Bush was virtually leveled as part of an "urban renewal" project in the 1960's. Much of the Bush's grid street pattern was obliterated in favor of the "towers in a park" public housing fashion of the time.

Some of the old Bush survives. The Italian Workmen's Club, established in 1912 is still there, and members still make their own wine. Fraboni's deli still serves up hot Italian sausage, locally made DiSalvo's red sauce and more. Temple Beth Israel is being refurbished. Longfellow School preserved and protected for decades by Meriter Hospital may soon get a new life as housing.

Now, through the Greenbush-Vilas Partnership, major institutions in the neighborhood are joining with neighborhood associations, the city of Madison and other partners to bring back the Bush. The urban renewal projects of fifty years ago and the bunker-like buildings along parts of Regent Street are nearing the end of their useful lives. It's time to reimagine and reinvent.

As Catherine Murray writes, "We can't bring back the old Bush. But we can honor its heritage and use its strong foundation to build on. Greenbush was like a tapestry of varied colors, with threads interwoven to create a picture and a reminder of an era...and when the tapestry began to fade...no one wanted to brighten its colors... except for the immigrants and their families who so carefully patterned their community from it to make it livable and to call it home."

FRANCESCA'S STORY

I am Francesca Martini and I was born and raised in Palermo, Sicily, in Italy. I dearly loved living in Palermo with my family and friends all near by. I loved the ocean and the singing of our own opera singer.

One day my husband Tony came walking into our house with terrible news. It was midday, and I was just setting out the noonday meal. As soon as Tony saw me, he said in a low voice, "We must leave Palermo".

I stopped short. "What do you mean, we must leave Palermo? What's got into you? This is our home. Everything and everyone we have ever known and loved is here. Why would we leave? Our families have been here for generations. You work hard to support us. Where would we go? How on earth would we manage?"

"I can only tell you," Tony replied, "that there has been some serious trouble.

When events come to light and the missing bodies are found, certain people will come looking for me, and they will be merciless if they find me. The only safely lies in getting to a place where I cannot be found."

"And where" I answered, "would that be, this side of the grave?"

Tony continued, "I've booked passage for us on a steamship bound for America.

The voyage will last 21 days, and steerage is the best

I could do. We will need to provide our own food. That's what we'll pack in our trunks. It will be hard, but we're young and we'll manage; when the ship docks in New York harbor, we can begin to live the rest of our lives."

"In New York City? Are you sure they'll let us in? We have no family there; we don't know a soul. We don't speak the language. You won't have a job. We'll be living on the streets!"

"We'll have to change our name," Tony continued. "From New York we'll go by train to Wisconsin. We have family in Madison. They will welcome us and see us right until we can stand on our own. In their letters to us they always mention the neighborhood they live in. It's full of Italians and is know as the 'Greenbush'. It won't be Palermo, but it will be the next best thing. We must be gone by tomorrow. We will be safe if we leave in time. There's not a moment to lose. We must hurry. We board the ship in the morning."

"Well," I thought, "do we just walk out the door, leave everything behind and say, 'that's that'? What about the children? What about the house? What about everything in it? What about the friends and relatives we will never see again? How on earth do you just walk away from everything you have ever known?"

I was dazed by the suddenness of what I was expected to do. It was as though the earth was falling away under my feet.

I had to leave my precious items that I used every day in our house, but I did take my mother's jewelry that she had given me and a small clock that I loved. Tony said my brother would say goodbye to our family and friends. He had asked all of our children to come with us, but the only ones that wanted to come were our son August, his wife Angelina, and their three children Samuel, Reiny, and Marcella.

Christina, aged 18, Vito, aged 17, Isabella, aged 16, Dominic, aged 15, and Stefano, aged 14 would stay in our house, and my parents would move in and take care of them, Tony said. It seems that Tony is planning all of this without my opinion, and this made me mad. Two of our children, Christina and Vito were planning to get married soon. I wouldn't even be there for them.

After my disturbing conversation with Tony, I finally found my voice and managed to put my thoughts together. Holy Mother of God, what was the problem? What sort of trouble was Tony in? How could it be so serious that we would have to leave Palermo? What on earth could he have done? Why will he not tell me?

Tony has never been in trouble like this before. Is there another woman? If there was, I think I would know. There are no secrets in Palermo. You can't even sneeze without word getting around town that you're coming down with a cold.

Our people have lived here since time immemorial. Our lives are here. Our way of living is here, not in some other country thousands of miles away. We're not that young anymore. We have our home; we've raised our children. Everything we have is here, not in some far off land.

But Tony keeps saying he's not safe in Palermo and never will be again. He's booked passage for us on a ship. He's bought two trunks and packed them with food for the journey. Where is he getting the money? We've never had much to spare at all. We've never had the kind of money Tony is spending.

So why won't he tell me what's going on? He says

there's no time, not a moment to lose; we'll have time on the ship, and we'll talk then. I want to talk to our priest, but Tony has forbidden even that. So where do I even begin? It sounds as though we are leaving forever.

If no one knows me, how will I ever matter to anyone again? Will our children be lost to us forever? Will we ever see them again? I'm their mother. This is disgraceful, and Tony will pay for it. I hope he will pay for it for the rest of his life. If he thinks he can wave a wand, and I will walk onto that ship without a care in the world and say goodbye to everything I've ever known and loved, he can think again.

I never thought our marriage vows of "love, honor and obey" would come to this. But without a way to earn a living, I have no choice. To top it all off, to preserve Tony's precious safety, we have to change our last name. I don't want to get on that ship. I don't want to go thousands of miles away. This is where we belong, and I want to stay right here!

I can't think about it now. I'll have to stop thinking while I get together the few things we can take with us. Tony says he has made all the arrangements. He has done all of that. He has arranged that nothing will ever be the same for us again. Am I supposed to admire him for that? If I could send him directly to hell I would, as hell is exactly where he belongs.

He tells me this will be a big adventure, and he has contacted his relatives to tell them we will be coming to Madison, Wisconsin where they live.

The next day, we got on the boat early in the morning, and the trip began. The first days were terrible. We were all seasick and I was still very angry. Why were we doing this?

I missed my children and I missed my house and town. I hated this boat! We were in steerage passage in the boat, which is the lowest part of the boat. I didn't imagine that we could be so sick. All of us. Space was extremely crowded and bunk beds were stacked from floor to ceiling. Water and fresh air were in short supply and privacy was nonexistent.

But gradually we adjusted to the motion of the boat and the sickness abated, and we were hungry once again. We had plenty to eat on the long 21-day voyage across the ocean, but many of the other families did not have enough food. I was proud of Tony for giving food to the others, and for trying to teach us a little English from books with lots of pictures and English words that he brought along.

A wife has to do what her husband wants of her, and I can't stay mad at Tony, the way he is helping everyone.

Tony made a deal with one of the officers on board to get an extra ration of water, and to use the galley for cooking a hot meal in the afternoon when the galley is free. How did he manage this? Did he bribe them? Where did he get the money?

So many of the people in the boat were Italian, and we became good friends by the end of the trip. Many went on to Madison, Wisconsin because we told them there were jobs there and a whole colony of Italians. Hope we are correct about that.

The ship's bells rang every two hours night and day to post shifts for the sailors.

Tony used the bells for a clock and put together a "Marriage Bed Corner" so that married couples could spend two hours together in privacy. He posted a list of all the couples and they all looked forward to this private time. During the trip two couples from steerage were married by the captain, and they had time in the Marriage Bed Corner. I wonder how many babies were conceived there.

There were several people on board that played musical instruments, and it was so much fun to sing the songs with them. We got to know people through these activities and had a lot of fun—adults and children alike. There were storytellers, too, and many of us told about our lives in Italy. Tears were shed when this happened.

We all decided that we would have a prayer meeting every night before we went to bed to thank God for getting us this far on our journey. Tony was a good organizer for these activities, and some people loved to pray and lead the group.

There were three deaths during our trip to America. The first one was a tiny baby who grew weaker and weaker. I think she had pneumonia because she had trouble breathing. Very sad. the other two deaths were an elderly woman who fell and didn't come around again. The man who died had health problems before he came on board, and he got worse and worse. The captain of the ship said some kind words and there were three burials at sea. These were very sober moments for all of us.

Finally, we saw the Statue of Liberty in the New York harbor. What a beautiful sight, and we all gave thanks to God for a safe journey.

When we arrived at Ellis Island, we were given food to eat. Some of the food was not good, indeed some of it was rotten meat and apple core pies. Thankfully the government put a stop to it when it was reported to them.

Many of the immigrants were so hungry that they ate everything handed to them. One woman ate a whole banana, not knowing the peel should not be eaten. She had never seen a banana before. American food was very different from what the immigrants were used to.

We worried about getting through the inspections at Ellis Island. There were many rumors about people being sent back to their country, and we were supposed to look healthy and happy. I am happy to report that all of us passed the tests, and we started our train journey to Madison, Wisconsin where —hopefully—our relatives would meet us.

The train ride was 19 hours from New York to Chicago, then another hour from Chicago to Madison. We rode through the big country of America. We saw cities, workmen, towns, wide open spaces, many farms and farm animals, and people who dressed differently from us and looked different. It was interesting, and kind of scary for all of us. We marveled at the beautiful and very large country and everything in it Would we ever be a part of this?

We live with the Pelliteris in Greenbush, a part of Madison, Wisconsin. Tony's relatives seem glad to see us, and they are very nice to all of us. We have two rooms in their house, and we all cook and make meals together. The house is clean, roomy, and bright, and I like it very much. Samuel's three children have cousins to play with and they all have chores to do.

Many people in the Bush are Italians, but there are other nationalities, too. They seem to get along, and all have jobs. The Catholic Church has classes for teaching English, and we all go. We speak English in the house, and so it was easy to learn the language.

The Pelliteris have a huge garden with vegetables, fruit

trees, and grape vines. We women take care of the garden and the men take care of the grapevines and make wine.

Tony got a job in a hardware store and he loved it. He had always been a fixer and builder, so the store was an answer to his dreams. People came to the store to buy, but also to socialize, with a chess table set up for all to use while drinking coffee. They had interesting conversations in the store, and friendships were made.

After a year at the Pelliteris we found a house that was reasonable. Where did Tony get the money for the down payment, I wondered. "I have been saving, and I finally got some money from our house in Italy from my brother," he said. After all those years, I had wondered if we would ever get money from the house that we all loved.

The house we bought was run down, and we had to do a lot of work to make it livable. The family painted, fixed things, cleaned, and got the yard in shape. Then we moved in, and we had another problem. We didn't have furniture for the house.

Through the relatives, hardware store, and the grapevine we made it known that we would do lawn work, clean houses, paint rooms, baby sit, and fix things in exchange for good solid "old country" furniture. We were able to furnish our house with barter. It was surprising to find good pieces of furniture in garages, attics and basements. We loved the old furniture for our house. We worked for months to get our house completely furnished, but it was worth it. We were all proud of our house and yard. We planted a big garden and grapevines.

Then came the horrific flu epidemic, and it was so ghastly that I hate to even talk or think about it. The flu took our son August, his wife Angelina, and their children Reiny and Marcella. Only our grandson Samuel survived the flu. We could not have a proper burial of our family. The authorities came and took the bodies away because they were contagious, and so we had our own family memorial service. Now, we have just Samuel from our family from Italy.

We also lived through the Great Depression, starting in 1929 in the United Sates.

Times were very tough for families and jobs were scarce. Most families did not have enough food to eat.

Things were bad in the Bush, too, but everyone had a huge garden (most converted grass lawn to garden) and people just got by.

Women canned vegetables, made sauerkraut out of cabbage, wrapped apples, carrots, rutabagas, turnips, onions and potatoes in newspaper and placed them in boxes in the cellar.

Tony had the hardware store, but most people could not pay their bills. Tony let his customers charge the vital items that they needed, and many of them never paid later when they could. It was a time when Tony decided he had to help people when he could.

Times were much worse in the west where there was a horrific Dust Bowl.

Farmers could not farm because of the Dust Bowl, and they moved on to other places to find work. There were no jobs, and families moved into houses with other families. There were many people living in one house. Most cities and towns had soup kitchens and that was the only food many people had to eat.

The Depression crash was in August 1929, and the depression lasted until March of 1933, although times were still tough. One hundred Wall Street men lost everything they had and jumped to their death in New York. Many others shot themselves because they, too, had lost everything.

Franklin Delano Roosevelt (FDR) was president and he was a hero in our house. He had a program called the New Deal, with many alphabet soup programs to help the poor and provide jobs to the men:

Civilian Conservation Corps (CCC)

Works Progress Administration

(WPA) Public Works Administration

(FWA) Farmer Relief Act (FRA)

Federal Arts Program (FAP)

Rural Electrification Administration (REA)

National Youth Administration (NYA)

Tennessee Valley Authority Dam Construction

These programs provided jobs for thousands and thousands of men and they were lifesavers for families. Men working under the WPA dug ditches by hand for sewer and water projects. These men probably had a lard sandwich for lunch and the work was very hard.

As a young boy, my grandson Samuel watched the men working with their patched-up clothes and holes in their gloves and he felt sorry for them. One day I had baked some cookies and they were cooling on a cookie sheet. Sam took the cookies and gave them to the working men. He was a hero! But I did not like it a bit. There were no cookies for our dinner that night.

SAMUEL'S STORY

My first memories are of living in Italy in our little corner of Sicily. I remember aunts, uncles, cousins and family friends who were such a big part of our lives. Family parties were boisterous and fun, with lots of good food and games. Bocci ball was my favorite.

My parents August and Angelina, my brother Reiny and sister Marcella were forever playing tricks on me, and our big extended family was close and got together often.

I also remember going to the market every day with my mother, and playing with the kids. Mother loved going there for the social part of it, and also to get fresh food for our meals. It was like a big celebration every day, with opera singers singing wonderful opera songs, and lots of fish, eels, octopus, vegetables, fruit—oh, the fruit. We all loved the fruit and it was a big part of our lives.

The market square smelled delicious, with bread baking in the communal ovens, and delicious sweet rolls and cookies in the bakery. I remember all of it.

But one day we hurried up and got our things together and got on a boat for America. I still don't know why this took place, but none of us wanted to leave Palermo. We didn't have time to think! We all went to bed that night packed up to go the next morning. I couldn't even say good-bye to my cousins, aunts, uncles and friends.

The boat was huge, and we lived in it for 21 days. Grampa Tony and Gramma Francesca helped us get through it all. We were all seasick for several days. So sick! After that, we hunkered down and learned some English and played games with other kids. We learned to play chess, and we had good food, thanks to Grampa. He had packed two trunks of food, so we had it pretty good. Some of the others did not have much food, and Grampa helped them whenever he could.

We were able to go up on the upper deck one hour a day, and that was the best time of the day. We had to be quiet and polite to everyone and we were! It was hard, but we did it because we loved to get out of the steerage part of the boat.

When we arrived in New York City and saw the Statue of Liberty, we were so thrilled and happy. Going through customs was scary, but we got through it. then we got on a train and went across the country, and that was an adventure.

The train stopped now and then, and Grampa bought us food. What a huge country! We passed through big cities and little towns, and much farm country. We saw cows, horses, sheep, pigs, oats, lots of birds that I have never seen before, but no ocean. There were lakes and rivers, but no ocean. We were all used to seeing the ocean, and we all loved it.

When we arrived in Madison, Wisconsin, it was a relief to get off the train and meet our relatives. They were so nice to us, and their house was so big and nice. I liked my cousins.

We lived with the Pelliteris for almost a year and

I know it must have been hard on them to have us all there. There were very gracious with us and such nice people, but we were happy to find a house to buy. We wondered where Grampa got the money for the down payment, but we loved having our own house.

Grampa Tony was so lucky to get a job in a hardware store here in the Bush. The owner is teaching Tony all about the hardware business and he loves it. Someday, I bet he will own a hardware store just like it.

My father August got a job in Oscar's Grocery Store, much like the store he had in Palermo. He was so happy to get the job and he worked hard. We kids helped teach him English, which we learned at school. Our Catholic school was a good school, but I got a little tired of going to Mass every day.

As I got older, I worked in Oscar's Store weekends, and I found that I really liked the store. Oscar and my father were both patient with me and taught me so much.

When I graduated from high school, I worked full time at the store, but then came the flu.

In 1918 there was a terrible flu epidemic all over the world. America was struck hard, and our family all had it. We were put in tents because the hospitals were full, and it was traumatic for all of us. I was so sick that I didn't know where I was and we didn't get much care because there were not enough nurses.

How were we ever going to get well? We were so weak, and we didn't care if we lived or died.

I saw a stretcher being carried out with a body on it. I couldn't see who it was, and I didn't know where my family members were. We could barely see or understand what was happening.

As I got a little bit better, I noticed a spider spinning her web way up high in the highest peak of the tent. I watched this with great interest. How many legs does a spider have? I wondered. What is the silky substance of the web like? How do they reproduce? Do they live as a family?

As the day went by, I started to talk to the man next to me. He started watching the spider spin her web too. "Do females or male spider spin webs?" I asked him.

Another man nearby entered the conversation and said he would ask his son to bring him a book about spiders.

Another stretcher was being carried out with a body on it. I wished I could see my family, but there were so many on cots in the tent.

The next day, the man in the neighboring cot had a book all about spiders. We all asked him to read information from the book and most everyone around us seemed interested too. This gave us something to think about.

Imagine our surprise when we found that there are 45,730 species of spiders in the world! The spider silk has chemical properties that make it lustrous, strong, and light and it is stronger than steel! Scientists have been trying for years to decode what gives the silk its strength and elasticity, but they are unsuccessful in finding these clues. They hope to be able to farm the material and use it for skin grafts, or to increase the strength of body armor. There are many ways a spider web could be used in our lives. Companies currently use spider silk for making shampoos and other cosmetics.

We read more and more about spiders, and we are

fascinated by what we have learned. A spider starts to spin its web at the outside and works its way in, attaching segment by segment with its legs creating concentric circles and ending in a center spiral of sticky silk that traps much needed prey for their food. The sticky stuff merely immobilizes the prey and the spider attacks the prey with their teeth and bite the thing to death. The spider's jaws are strong, and they get the food they need in this manner. Sometimes spiders eat their own webs when they are done with them as a way to replenish the silk supply.

Spider silk is made of connected protein chains that help make it strong and flexible. It is produced by internal glands, moving from a soluble form to a hardened form and then spun into fiber by the spinnerets on the spider's abdomen. Spider's multiple spinnerets and eight legs come in handy for web building.

Any individual spider can make up to seven different types of silk, but most generally make four to five kinds. Web building serves as both offense and defense because webs are used to catch prey for food, and also vibrations in the strands alert the spiders to predators.

Every spider species has its own preferred architecture, and some might be at home in the bottom of a paper cup, while others wouldn't touch that space.

I and the other patients around me are fascinated with information about the spiders, which are such an interesting part of our lives now. It has helped us heal and become a part of our living world. I still have a great interest in spiders to this day.

There came a time when I was getting stronger and I was eating more and I was able to leave the hospital tent. Tony and Francesca came to get me to take me home.

"Where are my parents, sister and brother?" I asked

There is no easy way to tell me that my parents, sister and brother are all dead. Tony and Francesca try to help me, but I have to do this on my own. I am now the only living person in my family. Francesca tells me that I will continue to live with them, and they love me and will help me get through this. I know that they both love me, and I'm happy that they are near me, but grief is a lonely and heartbreaking thing that I have to work through myself. I feel myself changing from a happy person to a quiet and thoughtful person.

In the end, when all the dead are counted, 675,000 Americans died, and 50 million died worldwide from the 1918 flu. Unbelievable.

Before the flu my father and I had been working in Oscar's store. Now Oscar gave me a job again in the store. Oscar treated me like his son, and I learned a lot about running a grocery store. I really think Oscar was grooming me to take over the store, looking back.

When the time came for Oscar to retire, he wanted me to have the store. Tony stepped in and paid the down payment, which I was thankful for. My grandparents were always there for me.

During the last year, I had been dating Rosita, who is beautiful and sweet. She is from the Bush and a customer of the store. That's how I met her. I can't believe how lucky I am! Rosita and I are married, and we have a great grocery store which we have renamed Martini's Market. Tony and Francesca both love Rosita, and they help us with the store. We live with Tony and Francesca and we are happy.

The store was pretty worn down, and we worked hard to paint, and upgrade the store We put in a new floor and turned it into a bright and sparkling store with lots of love and work.

Rosita and I are shy and quiet people, but we are getting acquainted with our customers and it's fun to joke around with them. We have good friends in the store.

Through the years we had six wonderful children, and Tony and Francesca have helped us with the kids. We work at the store six days a week, and we needed their help. We have Gino, August, Regina, Ernest, Tony and Anna Maria. As soon as they get older, they will all work in the store. Rosita's sisters take care of the children a lot.

I am so excited that Gino bought a lot right next to the church and turned it into a bocci ball field. We named it Martini Park. We all worked to level it and plant grass seed.

"Where did you get all the money for the field? "Carmen said.

"I've been saving it for a long time for just this thing," Tony said. "It's a good business project and the whole community can use it."

Living in the Bush is almost like living in Italy. Many people still speak Italian and we love Italian food and games. I love bocci ball and I play whenever I can at Martini Park, which we all work to keep well groomed. The women cheer us on when we play. Just like Italy. I am teaching my boys how to play bocci ball and they are picking it up fast. We now have bocci tournaments with many teams competing.

The years go by, and the kids grow up and now, after having the store for many years, I am retiring. Gino tells me that he will ask Carmen to be his wife, and I'm sure that together they will run the store as Rosita and I have done all these years. I'm happy that they want to buy the grocery store and keep it in the family. Tony is again stepping in to help with the down payment for the loan. What a great family we have.

ROSITA'S STORY

I am Rosita Martini. I was born in Italy and my family and I immigrated to Madison, Wisconsin to find a better life. We are a happy family, but poor, but we have a better life here than in Italy.

My father worked at a farm near Madison which raised tobacco and other crops.

The work was hard, but Dad was a tough Italian, and he was so happy to have a job outside in the fresh air. He was extremely loyal to his employer in a rough and tough way.

My mother was a busy lady with six children to care for, and her mother who lived with us. In those days, the mother of the family did all the housework: cooking, baking, cleaning, sewing, and knitting and taught the children how to get along with each other and still have fun in their lives.

Mother taught us games of all kinds, especially math games and card games where we had to think to play. We learned the states and all about them with a card game with information about the states. We all learned to respect each other and take care of each other.

We had a huge garden and we had to work in it. We planted, harvested, cleaned, canned, and prepared apples, pears, carrots, rutabagas and turnips for the winter by wrapping them in newspaper to keep them during the winter.

We had jobs to do every day, and it was no big deal to do them! We cheerfully did what my mother asked us to do. As we got older, we were expected to get jobs in stores or restaurants. We had to contribute to the family's financial support. We became independent and learned much from this lifestyle. It has helped all of us to be good citizens. My sisters are Maria, Patrice, Bettina, and Johanna, and my brother is Roberto.

I met Samuel in Oscar's Grocery Store in the Bush where we live. Sam was a young, handsome, energetic man who helped me to find my groceries when I came in. He told me after we were married that he loved me at first sight, and he followed me around the store when I came in. I learned that his family had died in the flu epidemic and I felt sorry about that. Such a nice young man.

He didn't ask for a date for months, and finally he asked me to go to a movie. I was surprised, but I said yes. We started dating, and we had such fun with my family and his. Both of us were out of school, and I worked at Monkey Wards (Montgomery Wards) as a clerk.

Sam introduced me to his grandparents, Tony and Francesca, and I loved them right away. Francesca told me that I was good for Sam, especially since he had lost his family to the flu. She said they worried about him, but now he was happy again.

We got married with a jolly and happy wedding with all our families there.

Everyone brought Italian food, and it was a happy day for us. We live with Tony and Francesca.

Tony helped us to buy the grocery store with money,

and helped with the paper work. Oscar retired and it is a miracle that we can buy the store. I never in the world thought my husband and I could own a store!

We loved the store, but it was run down. We worked to perk it up with paint and a new sign—Martini's Market—a new floor, and just generally new ideas. It was so much fun! The store was all ours!

Sam loved to play bocci ball, and I cheered him on at the games. Martini Park was well used by all of us in the Bush. Tony owned a great hardware store which had been successful from the beginning. Tony loved the store, where men congregated for cards and chess. The men solved many world problems there and had fun.

Our store had many bulk goods like cookies, oatmeal, vinegar (bring your own gallon jug), nuts, pasta, rice, beans and many more.

We started having children, with Gino, then Anna Maria, then August (named for Sam's father who died from the flu), Earnest, Tony, and Regina. We have six wonderful, but rough and tough Italianos who would work hard for each other. I have tried to calm them down, but I guess it's the nature of the beast!

We never knew what those unruly kids would do. One time in church Gino, who was four years old, said in a loud voice, "Hang on Jesus, you're going for a ride!" as he swung a rosary around and around during a very quiet time of the Mass. Everyone laughed—even the priest.

Father Danny came to the store one day and chuckled as he told us about Gino's first day of school. Father Danny said he asked the class if anyone could say the *Hail Mary*, and Gino was the only one to raise his hand. Then Father asked if anyone could say the *Our*

Father, and again Gino raised his hand and recited the *Our Father*.

Then Gino said, "You name it and I'll say it!"

They have fun and work hard, but they also get into trouble. Especially with the nuns at the Catholic school where they go. It seems Sam and I are always called into the office at school with one or the other.

My sisters take care of the children during the day when Sam and I work in the store. We in turn give them food from the store. It helps all of us. My sisters take our children swimming, ice skating, out for ice cream, to movies, and just take care of them. I am so thankful that we have this arrangement. Our kids love their cousins, and they have been lifelong friends to this day. We all live close to one another, so we can walk to each other's houses and have parties.

Where have all the years gone? Sam tells me that he wants to retire from the store. I can't believe it! He told me that Gino would like to buy the store, and it would be great to keep it in the family. Gino has worked at the store since he was little, and I know he loves the store. It looks like Carmen is going to be in the picture, and she would be great in the store with Gino. I hope they have children so we can take care of them I'd love to have grandchildren!

WORLD WAR II

In Europe, Adolf Hitler was gearing up to develop a world dominated by Germany. This was his dream, and it started in 1939. Our country was isolationist and didn't want to be involved in another war, but England was urging us to help fight Germany. We remained neutral.

Then on December 7, 1941 the Japanese Navy bombed Pearl Harbor in Hawaii and we lost 2,403 Americans. That was the straw that broke the camel's back.

The Sunday attack was completely unexpected, and the attack was horrific. Everyone in the United States was furious and violently angry at Japan. President Roosevelt had a Fireside Chat in the White House and we were at war! FDR said, "A day that will live in infamy!"

There were seven huge battleships with 1500 men on each one all lined up like ducks in a pond There were 89 other cruisers, destroyers and submarines at rest in the harbor. American aircraft were closely parked together at the airfield.

The Japanese bombed the aircraft first and strafed barracks and hangers with machine guns. The 181 Japanese fighters and bombers then bombed the seven battleships and other ships in the harbor. The whole terrible battle massacre took place in two hours, and 188 planes and 19 ships were destroyed, with 2,403 killed. The Japanese lost 29 planes and six submarines.

The Japanese sent the code signal "Tora, Tora, Tora" (Tiger, Tiger, Tiger) to tell the government that the surprise attack was successful.

America geared up the war machine: building fighter planes, ships and guns, and manufacturing ammunition and clothing for the armed forces and many more war products. Our young people were drafted into the Armed Forces and women stepped up and did the jobs that the men left. Rosie the Riveter was an example of a woman who riveted machinery after the men were gone. Women could do anything!

Our American scientists developed Penicillin, that would kill bacteria, from green mold. What a breakthrough this was. All the world wanted this drug, and it was a life- saver in the war and after the war.

We found out the Jewish people were being killed in Germany and Poland by the thousands. It turned out at the end of the war that millions of Jews were killed by the Germans. Some of the Jews came to our borders and we did not let them in! This is so shameful. The world was in a bad way. Americans thought immigrants would take jobs and houses away from Americans.

The European War of World War II ended in 1945. Then we still had to fight the Japanese war. By this time our boys were worn out and hated to think of going to the Japanese to fight them.

Our government had developed an atomic bomb, which was very secret. Our government warned the Japanese government that we had a terrible bomb that we would drop on Japan if they did not surrender. We urged them to surrender, but they would not.

We dropped the bomb on Hiroshima on August 6, 1945 and there was terrible destruction. The worst bomb in the history of the world. Again the American government urged the Japanese to surrender, and they again said no. Another atomic bomb was dropped on Nagasaki on August 9. Finally, after all that destruction Japan surrendered. The war ended September 1945.

More than 16 million American men served in the second world war, and there were nearly 300,000 deaths in battle and 115,000 other deaths in the war. 670,000 men were wounded in the terrible war. The three totals of the figures were three times greater than those killed or wounded in World War I.

GINO'S STORY

I, Gino Martini, grew up in the Italian Greenbush (the Bush) in Madison, Wisconsin. My family came from Italy, and they are rough and tough Italianos. Sam and Rosita, my parents, had a grocery store with everything from soup to nuts, and we all worked in the store as soon as we could walk and talk. There are seven children in our family.

My house that I grew up in was a Sears Roebuck Home that my family ordered from the Sears Modern Homes Catalog. We had indoor plumbing, central heating and electricity, which made our house very modern. There were 44 different models, with many different sizes and plans, ranging in price from $360 to $2,890. We bought our house in the forties, and it was a lot of money then. (A loaf of bread cost five cents in those days.) Our house was in the lower price range, with a big kitchen, living room, and bathroom downstairs and three bedrooms upstairs. There was a long porch in front, which we all loved, with a porch swing.

We had to have the cement work done, with footings and basement poured before the house came, and the cement had to "cure" for a length of time. Then the house was delivered, and the hard work began. Good thing we had lots of help, because it was a tremendous job putting it all together. One of our relatives was able to read the blueprints and understand how it all fit together. He was a hero to us.

Our house was shipped by railroad car and then trucked to our site. It weighed 25 tons with over 30,000 parts, besides plumbing and electrical and heating systems. Plasterboard products were developed and provided as an alternative to plaster and lath walls. Also asphalt shingles had been developed and were safer for fires. The kitchen and bathroom were very modern, and we were thrilled with the house.

Our family got together and put the house up, after figuring out how to do it. There were instructions, and all the precut timbers were numbered. With all those numbered pieces of lumber it was like putting together a giant jigsaw puzzle.

The men in our family and some friends worked hard to figure out how to put the framework of the house up beginning with the first floor, and then the upstairs. Good thing we had nice sunny weather that month in the summer we built the house. Our men worked at their jobs all day, and then worked on the house until dark every night. Weekends were all spent working on the house, and everyone was exhausted.

Our family made a deal with an electrician and a plumber. They evaluated the work to put electricity in the house and plumb the house. Then our family women worked for them in various ways to pay for these services. The men could not work because they worked on the house all the free time from their jobs, so it was up to women to provide services in exchange for these two jobs.

The women cooked, baked, babysat, cleaned houses, mowed lawns, worked in gardens, and so on. In this way, everyone in the family contributed to the building of the family house.

Sears offered a mortgage at 6% to 7% interest, which we took advantage of. During the Great Depression, Sears did away with the mortgages because so many could not pay. Sears had their own lumber mills and sash and door companies. These precut and prebuilt houses were the first of their kind.

We didn't build a garage because we didn't have a car. We walked all over, and if we wanted to go someplace farther away we took the bus. Madison buses were fun to ride on, and we sometimes rode the bus just for the fun of it.

When we finally moved into our new home, and we were all settled in, we invited the whole community to an open house party so that all could see our new home. There were so many people that we moved some of the activities into the street with music and dancing on into the night. Of course, we had wine and food in abundance, and a good time was had by all, with people of all ages dancing and having fun.

This was the first Sears House built in the Bush, but not the last. Many families came to visit and ask for our advice about building their own Sears House.

I am sorry to say that my brothers and I were known as little hellions in our neighborhood. My sisters all stood up for us and helped us out of jams so our parents would not hear about it.

A few weeks after we moved into our Sears House, my brothers and I were watering the new grape vines and apple trees when we decided to play "fireman." We pretended that our next-door neighbors had a fire in their house, and we had to put it out. We sprayed water from the hose into the open windows and had fun "putting out the fire."

Our neighbors started to yell and scream at us, and we ran into our house. Our mother couldn't believe that we had done that, and we had to go with her to apologize, and then to clean up the water all over the room. From that time on, we were known as the naughty bad boys of the neighborhood! Our sisters didn't get us out of that one. I didn't think we had done something that bad. We were just having fun! My mother said, "What a way to meet our new neighbors!"

People in the Bush also said that the Martini kids were all smart and clever. We all played chess and lots of other games, along with soccer, ice skating, swimming and baseball, and we all loved bocci ball.

My older brothers always played tricks on us. They were pretty nasty with their creative trickery, but we never told our parents about these actions. We knew that it would be worse if we told on them.

One time my big brother said to me, "Shut up or I'll cut off your head and throw it in your face!" I wondered and wondered how that could happen.

Our house was always full of kids playing games and having fun. We always had a lot of food in the house, and our friends loved that! We had the only Monopoly game in the neighborhood, and we played a lot of games on rainy days.

We were all taught to get along with customers in our store. We had to be polite to all, and this was hard for us to learn. But learn we did, because our parents forcefully demanded that we all treat our customers with respect, or we wouldn't have a house to live in or food to eat. That was a strong argument for us to behave. There were many grocery stores in the Bush, and there was fierce competition.

We went to St. Joseph's Catholic Church, right in our neighborhood from K through 8th grade. It was hard for me to work hard in school because the nuns were so hard on me and my brothers. Do you suppose that was because we were so troublesome and annoying? It always seemed to me that the nuns liked the girls better than the boys.

I met Carmen in grade school, and I fell in love with her. Carmen didn't pay any attention to me, and I was crushed. I worked hard to get her attention, but to no avail. I dreamed of her constantly, but she wouldn't even speak to me. It was a horrible time of my life.

After grade school we both went to Central High School, and Carmen still would not even talk to me. One day, Carmen watched as I defended a small boy named Adam, who was bullied by a big kid in the school. I was furious, and I shoved the big bully to the lockers. "Why don't you bully me, you little twerp? If I ever see you bullying this kid again, you'll have to deal with me and my friends. Do you get this?" Adam was so relieved he worshipped me after that. It was embarrassing.

From that day forward, Carmen was interested in me, and I was in heaven. We started dating, went to Prom together, movies, and other places. I describe Carmen as snazzy-zazzy. Because of Carmen I did well in school, and I was in basketball and baseball, and also plays, because Carmen was in plays.

Adam always came to me for advice, and one day he asked me if he should ask Ellen to a dance. "Hell no," I said. "She has a boyfriend who is the jealous type."

"Who should I ask, then?" Adam said.

"How about Christina? She's a nice girl, and I think you would like her," I said. As it turned out, Adam and Christina went to the dance together, and fell in love.

I became their best buddy. Now Adam really was a pest! But in a nice way.

Carmen and I both loved living in the Bush, and we went to dances at the Italian Workman Club and Turner Hall. Everyone went to the dances, and we all went out to the restaurants there, and the movies. We swam in the summer, and ice skated in the winter at Brittingham Park. Carmen and I loved the same things.

There were Jewish, German, Black, Irish and of course Italian people living in the Bush. We all got along well, and we all helped each other when we could. There were many festivals, concerts, family doings and school activities. It wasn't Utopia, but for the most part, I loved it there.

Then came urban development. In order to widen the streets, houses had to be torn down, and also our church was torn down. These houses had families living in them for generations. Some of the people stayed on their porches and protested until the bulldozers came and knocked the houses down. It was a sad day in the Bush.

Eminent Domaine had the day.

Families had to find another house to live in, and sometimes it was far away from the Bush. Our family house and store were safe from the wrecking ball, but many others were not.

When my father retired, I got a loan and bought the store. After a year or so of "going with" Carmen, I took her to Picnic Point and got down on my knees. I proposed, and miracle of miracles she said yes. I was in heaven.

Our wedding was the social event of the year, and everyone came. Now we had the store and I had my dream wife.

We have four beautiful daughters and one wonderful son. Our daughters are spunky and interested in everything, but our son Michael is interested only in music and dance. Everyone loves Michael—all of his teachers, all of our family—and I think Carmen and the girls have spoiled him rotten.

I always wanted Michael to go out for sports and go hunting and fishing but he never wanted to. The girls say, "Let him do what he wants to do!" Our priest wanted Michael to become a priest, but he wasn't interested in that, either. I am sorry that I have called him a God-damned wimp because I know that he felt terrible about that. Why, oh why did I call him that?

Now Michael has a degree at the U in music and dance, which he worked very hard to get. What kind of a degree is that? What kind of a job will he get with that degree? Imagine! A degree in music and ballet!

There were many grocery stores in the Bush, but ours was very successful. Some of the stores sold moonshine, which they made illegally. My family did not do this. I turned out to be a pretty good store owner. My father had taught me well.

Carmen worked with me, and we are a good team. She knows that I idolize her, and when our children came, I idolized them too. I can't believe that I am this lucky

Our store was in Spaghetti Corners with many other

stores and restaurants. I had a nice display of cookies in bulk in six boxes with see-through doors. I placed it right in front of the counter so that a person could not reach inside and take a cookie. This was a popular item in the store, and we sold many, many cookies There were sugar cookies, ginger cookies, molasses cookies, spice cookies, chocolate cookies and bran cookies Each cookie was four cents. There was also a penny candy counter with a variety of penny candy.

Our store charged groceries to almost all of our customers. At the end of the month, families would pay the bill and we would give them a bag of candy for the family. Each family had an account book with their last name on it, and we put the books in a rack in alphabetical order.

Every day customers would call us and order groceries, and we would deliver them to their door. All the grocery stores in the Bush delivered groceries every day, and they were all open from eight to five and closed on Sundays.

One day a farmer came to the store and he had some nice-looking apples to sell. I had three empty barrels in the cellar, and I bought enough apples to fill the three barrels. The farmer carried burlap bags of apples down the stairs until they were filled. I paid the man and he went on his way.

We sold the apples, and everyone said they were the best apples we had ever had! After using the apples in the first and second barrel, we moved on to the barrel in the far corner and discovered that the farmer had tipped the barrel upside down and just had a layer of apples on the top of the barrel. He had cheated me! I wish that I knew the man's name and where he lived.

The years went by, and one day my friend Gregory asked me if I would sell the store to him and his family from Italy. I said NO. When I told Carmen she said, "Let's think about this. We would not have to worry about food spoiling and produce getting old. I think we would be better off with a store of arts and crafts. This is a coincidence that Gregory wants to buy the store. I know of a building on State Street that looks pretty good, and it's for sale. It's been vacant for a while, but it has potential."

I said NO NO NO. But everyone knows that Carmen always gets her way with me. Carmen made an appointment to go and see the building, and I finally said Yes. I could see at once that the building was solid and had potential. I hated to admit it, but Carmen was right!

We sold the grocery store to Gregory and his family and bought the building on State Street. Carmen did all the paperwork, she's very good at that, and we started work on the building.

We had enough money to buy the building from the sale of the store, but we needed a loan to buy stock for the store. I had met a man from Mexico, Jose, who told me about the little town he lived in that had such creative artists. He said no one knew about them, and they had many items to sell. I hoped he was telling me the truth.

I flew down there, and he was right. There were so many artistic people living there who had learned how to make pottery, ponchos, handmade woven Llama wool items, and jewelry. What a find!

I decided to buy a truck, and I bought a truckload of beautiful art pieces that were stunning and delightful. I was sure Carmen would love them for the store. Jose was surprised that I bought so much, and the whole town thanked me.

In the meantime, Carmen and the girls were working hard cleaning, painting, and sewing curtains. They worked so hard, but I think they loved it. All the girls were excited about the store, but Sherry was especially excited about it. She and Carmen went to New York and found gorgeous lines of clothing and jewelry. They seem to have a knack for finding good buys and smart fashions.

The store will be called "Martini's Boutique." I hope to hell it is successful.

My buddies and I go to the Knights of Columbus meetings together and play poker afterwards. We complain that the stakes are too low and are uninteresting, so we decide to go to my house and play poker every Tuesday night in the recreation room.

It's a B.Y.O.B. deal, and Carmen always bakes something and has munchies.

The rest of the family always finds something to do away from home on Tuesday nights because it's always so noisy and boisterous.

Aaron is an attorney, Carson is a teacher, and Mark has a big house and a big building supply company on the West Side. Mark is aggressive and wants to raise the bids all the time. He has family money and is wealthy, but the rest of us want to keep the stakes low.

One night Mark says, "Let's make the game interesting. I have a wonderful house in Middleton that I would love to bet on."

"The stakes are 'way too high for us," we all say.

"No, no, no. I would not gamble and risk losing my house".

"I have the biggest house of all and the most risk," Mark says. "Let's just think about it."

Then he says, "Let's play 5-card draw poker with deuces wild, and we can raise the bet to no limits."

"Are you in? I'll call after all have bid or folded," Mark says. Mark wins $50 and everyone moans and goes home.

The next Tuesday night is a snowy December night and Mark is feeling lucky. We are all in a good mood and drinking lots of beer.

"Let's make the game more interesting, and the next hand could be a game changer," says Mark. "Aaron, draw up an agreement that the winner of one of these games will win a house. Are you with me?"

Aaron says, "That would be nonsense One would win big and the other would lose everything. I won't write up a legal agreement!"

"Don't be crazy," says Mark. "Nobody has to do it. Just write up the contract just in case one of us wants to do it,"

Aaron finally writes up a contract, and we all sign it reluctantly.

It is Mark's turn to deal, and he is amazed. He has a royal flush. He had never had one before. Everyone but myself folds, and Mark says, "Are you in for the house deal? If I win I get your house, and if you win you get my house Do we have this straight?"

"Yes," I agree. I am thinking, what if Mark has five jacks, queens, kings or aces?

My five nines will not win. What are the odds of that happening?"

It is the final showdown and Mark has a royal flush. "I've never had a royal flush before. Do I win your house Gino?"

"Sorry, Mark. I have five nines—four nines and a deuce, and deuces are wild.

Five nines beats a royal flush."

Mark says, "%$#@&*%$! I can't believe you have won over a royal flush. It's really amazing. How am I going to tell Lois and my girls?"

"This was your idea and you dealt the hand. This was so stressful, I don't think I will ever play poker again," I said.

That is how I won a big beautiful house on the West Side of Madison, with a huge well-groomed lawn, and that is why Mark and I are arch enemies and there are no more Tuesday night poker games.

Our family all love "one-liners." My one-liner:

"I got some batteries that were given out free of charge."

CARMEN'S STORY

I grew up in Greenbush, an Italian part of Madison, and I have deep roots here. My family lived in a charming house on Regent Street, not eloquent but very nice and roomy. We lived near St. Joseph's Catholic Church and school and the church was a big part of our social life. I took piano lessons from the nuns, we all went to dinners there, rummage sales, youth sports, and many more activities. The kids in our family all went to St. Joseph's school down the block.

There are many grocery stores in the Bush, but we go to Martini's. Sam and Rosita own the store, and our family and theirs are good friends. Sam and Rosita both came from Italy.

Our family has Tortellini's Restaurant at Spaghetti Corners, with many other Italian restaurants. It's a crossroads of Italian businesses in the Bush. As soon as I was old enough, I had to work in the restaurant, and it was good experience for future jobs. Our food was so good, but we kids always wanted to go to Bunky's Restaurant. Guess the grass is always greener on the other side of the road.

My parents were always busy working in the store, so we kids went to our aunt's houses when we were little. We are so lucky to have aunts, uncles, and cousins who love us and take care of us. We have so much fun with them.

St. Joseph's school years were mostly fun, even though some of the nuns were hard to please. For the most part it was okay. My sisters and I had it pretty good, but it seems that nuns like girls better than boys. I didn't get too many slaps on the hands with a ruler.

I went to Central High School and I was in everything fun in the school. Band, cheerleading, chorus, forensics and debate. We didn't have girls sports, though. I was mad about that.

I dated a few boys in high school, but when Gino helped Adam one day, a boy who was being brutally bullied, I looked at Gino as a hero. I felt so bad for Adam. He was a small, nice boy, and the bully really had hurt him so much. I looked at Gino in a different way after that.

We started dating, and I never dated anyone else, and I knew that Gino would do anything for me. We had so much fun together. We went to loads of parties, both in school and with our families. We went swimming in the summer at Brittinghan Park, ice skating in the winter on the lake, all the games at school, and get-togethers with our families. I feel lucky that our families are so much fun.

Both of our families loved word games. We had contests for the best and mostclever word phrases. I won one day with, *"You can tune a piano, but you can't tuna fish."*

Gino won one day with, *"I know a guy who's addicted to drinking brake fluid, buthe says he can stop any time."*

GG Francesca had one. *"Haunted French pancakes give me the crepes."*

When Gino's father retired, Gino got a loan and bought the grocery store. It was a huge thing that was carefully planned and drafted to the smallest detail by Gino and his parents. He was lucky to get a loan that he could handle, and he worked very hard in the store. His father taught Gino how to run the store and it paid off for Gino.

After a time, Gino proposed to me at Picnic Point on beautiful Lake Mendota. It was so romantic, and I accepted. Our wedding was the highlight of my life.

As our children were born our families helped with babysitting until they were old enough to help in the store. Our days at the store were long and I really appreciated what our families did for us. My sisters were especially good to all of us. Our kids loved them and their cousins and learned so much from them. My sisters and brother didn't have to pay much for food from our store, and it was a good plan for all of us.

Our children are all beautiful, of course! They are fun and smart, too! Michael has been an altar boy and active in school. Gino wants him to work with him and go hunting and fishing, but Michael does not seem interested. He is very musical, playing the cello and piano, and he sings in the chorus and takes dance lessons. Gino says he's a "God-damn wimp." He blames it all on the girls and me. We all love him so much, but so does Gino. I think Gino will be sorry he called him this name sometime.

Michael has earned a degree in Music and Dance at the University of Wisconsin and has auditioned at the Ballet School of Dance in New York City. I really hope he gets it, because he wants it so badly. Gino does not know about this.

Olive is our oldest and is a Home-Econ teacher and is also a fine seamstress. Shehas always been talented and smart, and she is deliciously beautiful. Olive has always had friends at the house and is interested in everything One of her one-liners is, *"Stayed up all night to see where the sun went, and then it dawned on me"*

Ginny is classy and stunning and is a surgical nurse at UW Hospital. Doc Sophie has chosen Ginny to be on her neural surgical team, which is quite prestigious. Ginny is flattered that she was asked to be a part of that team.

Sherry has a degree in Home Econ and is now starting a catering business. She is another beauty, but she says she is a plain Jane compared to her sisters. I think she is just as pretty as the others, but Sherry thinks she is fat! She is not fat!

Bubbles got her nickname when she had a Halloween costume with bubbles all over her body, and the name has stuck with her. Gino says the name Bubbles Martini is great. Her real name is Alayna. She is a music teacher at Georgia O'Keefe Middle School. Like her sisters, she has fun wherever she goes, and she is gorgeous. Even if I do say so!

St. Joseph's Church has our Italian festival, which is always a gloriously fun and delightful two-day affair. The stores and restaurants in the Bush close those two days because everyone is at the festival. The food is so good. Women of the parish work for days preparing great spaghetti sauce, chicken, crusty bread, salads, and baked goods. People come from all over Madison to buy the delectable goods.

My favorite cookie is the fig-filled ones that melt in

your mouth. Another favorite is sesame seed cookies, that are crunchy and delicious. Nucatole with almonds is another cookie that I always love at the festival. Baked Pasta Milanesa is a great Italian dish. Pasta e Fagioli is another of my favorites, and it makes my mouth water!

There are games of chance with a roulette wheel (gambling is illegal, but no one seems to worry about this. After all, it's for the church!) There are many games for the kids with prizes. They all love the running games and bean bag games. The gunny sack races are fun, too.

At the beer tent, there were many, mostly men, who visited and drank and just had a good time. We women watched at a distance and were ready to take our men home when it was time. I noticed that Gino was having a really good time. He asked to borrow a scissors from behind the bar, and I saw him cut off neckties of three men before I could get to him.

"What the heck are you doing? Are you out of your mind?' I asked him.

"I just wanted these guys to be comfy and to take off their ties. What's wrong with that?" Gino said.

"Come with me, Gino. I want to talk to you," I said.

"Oh, Carmen. I'm having such a good time with all of my friends. Do I have to?" "Yes, you have to. We are going on a little shopping trip."

"I don't want to shop," Gino said. "Come on, don't be a child," I said.

"Gino, did you notice that the three men whose ties you cut off are our best customers? We are going to buy ties for those three men. Don't say another word!" I told him.

"Oh, my God. What the hell was I thinking of? Hope

they don't get mad at me!" Gino said.

"We are going to buy three of the nicest ties we can find, and hope they really like them. Let's get going."

Thank God the three friends liked the ties and remained our customers. There is so much competition for grocery stores in the Bush. We have to be really careful.

The Fourth of July was another big day in the Bush. Once again the women cooked and baked for days before the celebration. The food stands were amazing. One had spaghetti and meatballs and ravioli. Another had American hamburgers and hot dogs. Still another had fish fries, and of course there was a huge ice cream stand.

There were games and races with prizes for the children and a merry-go-around was brought in for the day at the church grounds.

Martini Park, right next to the church, is groomed for bocci ball, and the men are chomping at the bit! Women do not play. The grass is mowed by the men players, and they take turns making sure that the grounds are ready for the play. The field size is about 90 feet by 9 feet, and should be smooth, without bumps.

There are two, three or four on a team, with two teams. They take turns throwing the round wood balls and try to get close to the jack ball. The ball closest to the jack ball wins the point. Later on, bocci balls could be made of metal, baked clay, or plastic, but the original bocci ball was made of wood. The game is a cross between bowling and shuffleboard.

One year the Fourth of July was on a Friday, and because Catholics could not eat meat on Friday, Father

Danny announced, on the Sunday before, a special dispensation from the bishop. Catholics were allowed to eat meat at the church celebration food stands for that one day.

Gino told Father Danny that he had a very important question to ask him. Gino said, "What if I bought a hamburger on the church grounds and, still eating it, walked off the church grounds. Would I go straight to hell if I dropped dead?"

"Gino, you are incorrigible! No one but you would ever think of that scenario," said Father Danny. With that he walked off, but I could see that he was laughing.

All the money from the day went to the church, including that from the roulette wheel. Some of the policemen were there playing roulette while whey were off duty. There was a big bingo game going on in the church basement, too. It seemed like the volunteers were having just as much fun as the others. A good time was had by all.

As the years go by, Gino's friend Gregory asks Gino if he would sell the grocery store to him and his family from Italy. His parents had a store in Italy, and they really want a grocery store like Martinis.

Gino said, NO NO NO! But when he told me about it, I said, "This is a huge coincidence. This is meant to be. I know a store on State Street that is for sale, and it would be a great investment. It's kind of run down, but it's a good solid building, and close to the Capital. "Just think, Gino," I said, "we wouldn't have to worry about food spoiling anymore!"

Gino doesn't even want to think of it. But I take him to see the store, and he has to admit that it has potential. Gino says he will think about it, and I know I will get my way! Eventually Gino says he will look at the store. So, I arrange to have the seller show us the property. We talk about price; I get the store appraised and hire an inspector to come and inspect everything. Then I ask about the gas, heat, electricity, water, sewer and taxes. The building is sound, but it needs paint, tender loving care and upscaling. We finally agree on price and buy the building on State Street.

We meet with Gregory and his family and reach an agreement about price of the grocery store. They happily agree to take all the stock and the store is sold. Gregory and his family are the happy owners of the grocery store.

Martini Boutique will have handmade sweaters, scarves, hats, afghans, jewelry, clothing, artwork, toys, candies and other beautiful items. "Just think, Gino," I said. "we will both work in the store and you can go on buying trips to your friend Jose in Mexico."

We are all excited about having a store with so many beautiful things to sell. We will all make it work.

Gino is excited to go to Mexico. Years ago, he met Jose through the grocery store. He's from a little town in southern Mexico, and he has told Gino about the talented artists that live there who have learned their skills from their families. When Gino came home with his truckload of handmade items he said, "Carmen, I hate to say this, but you were right about buying the store on State Street, and I love going to Mexico."

Meanwhile, the girls and I paint, sew curtains, and generally remake the store. It is hard work, but we all love it. Sherry especially loves the store, and we collect hand- knit or crocheted afghans, hats, scarves, sweaters, jewelry and homemade candy. It seems that the Bush has talented artists and homemakers. One wall in the back will be drugstore items, such as Tylenol and vitamins. I am told that one wall will bring in more profit than the other merchandise.

Sherry and I went to New York for a buying trip and we found a line of very different and beautiful clothes. Sherry is really clever at selecting unusual and colorful clothing.

In our family we always had music. We played music in the grocery store, and at Martini Boutique we play music too. In the new store, we play mostly classical music, and our customers love it. It puts them into the mood for shopping, and they feel good about themselves.

We put up fliers all over the Capital Square announcing our Grand Opening of the Martini Boutique. We are off and running.

The first week is exciting, but not too many customers. Slowly, but surely the people will be coming, we hope, It takes a lot of time for people to find a new store and we all hope and pray that it is successful.

Gino loved to play poker, and he and his buddies often played poker after the meetings of the Knights of Columbus at the church. They decided that they wanted to play more often with higher stakes, so they formed the Tuesday Night Poker Club, which met in the rec room at our house. We all found something to do on Tuesday nights when they played. They were very loud and boisterous.

Gino won a house in Middleton playing poker.

He insisted that we all move into the house in

Middleton, on the West Side. It is a wonderful house, but we all love living in the Bush, and we all love our house. Gino insisted, but I said No. Gino told me that if we would move he could pay off the debt at the bank from the sale of our house in the Bush, and we would have a great house to live in.

After agonizing on it for a while, I said yes. Thank God all the kids had grown up in the Bush, and they all had degrees from the University of Wisconsin.

We moved into the house in Middleton and sold our house in the Bush. Our furniture did not "fit" the house and we went antique hunting for furniture. We paid off the debt and Martini Boutique was now ours, lock stock and barrel. It felt good.

One day two men from the IRS came to our house looking for Gino He wasn't home and I asked them what they wanted him for. They said they wanted to question him about income tax from last year. I asked questions about it, and they said it had to do with our house in Middleton. They came back two other times and Gino was not there both times. I told them about the wedding coming up and they wrote down the date.

When I told Gino about the IRS men he said, "Don't worry about it. I had my friend Steve appraise the house, and I paid tax on it according to that figure." He looked concerned, though, and he said he thought that his "good friend and buddy Mark" probably had something to do with it.

"I will deal with it" he said. Maybe Mark will have the last laugh! I'll ignore it and maybe it will go away."

I belong to the Raging Grannies of Madison, and GG Francesca does, too. We sing all over. We are liberal and try to get our message across with humor, as we dress in costumes that are silly and outrageous. We traveled to Washington, D.C. twice and have gone to New York City once for peace rallies. We have also gone to Chicago, Milwaukee, Oshkosh and many other places to sing our protest songs. I have been in Raging Grannies for 11 years, and the Grannies are the best friends I could ever have. Beside that, they think like I do.

My good friend and Raging Granny, Bianca was flamboyant and lively. She was a retired professor of Women's Studies at the UW, and she had the confidence to be outrageous with her long, wavy hair and bright, gaudy clothes. It was always fun to be with Bianca because she was never afraid to say what she believed in. She was a fierce believer in women's rights, and she wrote the lyrics of a song that is very clever, and we loved to sing it.

Bianca was eccentric even before she was old and eccentric! There are so many Grannies like her who are experienced and have self-assurance gained from their professional lives. I feel so fortunate to be a part of this interesting and worthwhile group, where we voice our opinions with singing and peaceful demonstrations.

I will never, ever vote for a Republican! Their philosophy is to always help wealthy people and corporations through cutting their taxes. They think it will "trickle down to the masses," but it has been proven that they are wrong. It has never happened. The Democratic philosophy is geared to help the poor and middle class with health care, public schools, clean air, clean water, more research for health care, more money for universities, and better housing for the masses. We must all vote intelligently and know the voting records of the candidates.

My first protest march was when I was in my 80's, when Governor Walker took away collective bargaining for teachers in Act 10. Governor Walker also cut taxes for the wealthy, stopped the train transportation plan that the former governor had put in place, and stopped the locomotive factory that was already in place in Milwaukee that would have added hundreds of jobs there. The governor was not receptive to clean air and clean water because big business would have to pay more! I could go on and on. This is why Raging Grannies protest.

The Grannies sang their songs and marched in peaceful protest during Governor Walker's regime of bad government and mistakes. Several Grannies were arrested and handcuffed and had to go to trial. The peaceful protests were all legal and we had permits to march, but Walker's bullies persisted. Lucky for us we had three retired attorneys in our group of Grannies After several court hearings they were found not guilty. In America, we are permitted to protest.

As our children and grandchildren grew older, I volunteered at the public school and eventually got a job as a part time aide in the library. I loved the job and loved the teachers I worked with. It was fun to get to know the students, and I tried to help them when I could. Some kids have a hard time in school.

Now I have two partial plates in my mouth and I have just had a prescription from my doctor to get a walker, because I have a balance problem. I refuse to call my wonderful walker "Walker" because Governor

Walker was such a buffoon, and because he did so many horrific things as governor. I call my walker "Elinor" because Eleanor Roosevelt was an idol for me.

GG Francesca always had a story to tell and I heard them all many times. GG Tony had a friend, Rudy, who had a meat market. GG Tony went to visit him one day and he asked Rudy to wrap up a big package of cheap pork ribs and mark the package Llama ribs—$12.00. GG Tony brought the meat package home, and GG Francesca was horrified.

"You paid $12 for these Llama ribs?" she demanded. "What are they? $12 is enough to feed us for three meals." There were eight of them, and GG really had to watch her money to put food on the table. "How do you cook Llama ribs?" she asked.

Rudy had told GG Tony that you brown them and then bake them slowly in barbecue sauce, so that's what she did.

They were delicious. GG Tony said, "Even though they were so expensive, it was nice to have something special."

That night, GG Francesca went to the Homemaker's Club and she told everyone about the Llama ribs that GG Tony had bought at Rudy's. Everyone wanted to try them, so the next day many women went to Rudy's Store and asked for Llama ribs. Of course, Rudy had to tell them about the prank GG Tony had pulled on GG Francesca. GG Francesca loved the whole thing.

GG Tony's one-liner was, *"Did you hear about the fellow whose entire left sidewas cut off? He's all right now."*

MICHAEL'S STORY

I am the youngest child in the Martini family. I have four great sisters and I love each and every one dearly. My wonderful parents dote on me and I appreciate all that they have done for me. We have many, many aunts, uncles and cousins who live close by in the Bush. I love all the family get-togethers we have, and all the activities here in the Bush.

At Halloween, all the stores in the Bush gave out candy to the Bush kids. The kids had homemade costumes made by their families, and it was a rollicking fun experience for the whole community.

One year my family helped me concoct a costume, a spaceman. Mother used a colander with wire antenna on top for the hat, and a shimmering silver suit that had a belt with reflectors glued on it. GG Francesca loaned me "spaceman's gloves" that went up to my elbows, and a flashing flashlight. I was the envy of the boys! I know my costume was the best of the year.

We all collected afterwards and compared notes on the best treats. Some stores gave out candy, some gum, some apples, but the best were always from GG Tony at his hardware store. He scanned catalogs all year for the best treat he could find, and it was usually a clever game or toy. We all went to him first to see what he had that year.

Most people in the Bush could not afford to buy candy or treats for the kids, so this took their place. Some families made cookies, but most of the houses were dark, which meant the kids would not "trick or treat" there. I remember having a paper bag with many, many treats in it. It was such an adventure to go from store to store and see all the costumes of my friends. It was quite wild, I must say.

We took our bags of goodies home and hid them from our sisters and brothers.

We didn't get much candy in those days, so this had to last us for a while!

I remember the Christmas when I was 9 years old we all stayed up and sang Christmas carols with lights on the tree and decorations all over the house. We had cookies out for Santa Claus, and we were all excited about Christmas the next day.

Finally, we were sent off to bed, and my parents put all the gifts and toys under the tree. We kids all dreamed about the presents we would be getting the next morning.

In the middle of the night there was a very loud noise downstairs. I heard my parents run down the stairs, and shriek and yell, and we all ran down to see what had happened. The ceiling had fallen down all over the Christmas tree. There were pieces of ceiling all over the tree and room. Gifts were covered with ceiling pieces. I started to cry and there was pandemonium. We were all in shock!

Mother was crying too, and we all thought Christmas was going to be horrible this year. How could this happen? But Dad saved the day. He said, "OK, let's get our gifts out from under and put them in the dining room.

We won't let this make our Christmas bad. We are going to have fun right now, in the middle of the night. We will never forget this Christmas, and it will be lots of fun.

"Each one of you take your gifts and put them on the dining room table, and Mother and I will clean them off. We are going to have our Christmas party right now, and then we will go to our relatives houses like we had planned, and just leave the mess in the living room. We will clean it up after Christmas but we will not worry about it now.

"So—let's pass out the presents and have fun. Do not even look in the living room, and let's put Christmas music on. It looks like Santa Claus came already, and we will have a great party."

None of us will ever forget that Christmas, and we all got the best presents that year. I got a Chemistry set with a microscope that I had always dreamed of having, and all of us had a wonderful Christmas in spite of the mess. After Christmas we all helped clean up the mess, and our relatives came and helped, too. Now we had a new ceiling in the living room and everything was back to normal.

My childhood was full of activities with my family. Our church was the social highlight of our lives. Easter was an important holiday in the Church, and we all gave up something we loved in the six weeks of Lent before Easter. One year, I gave up listening to my favorite radio show, which was a hard thing to do.

Little Orphan Annie was my favorite, and it was terrible to listen to the kids in school talk about what Annie was doing in the show. The next year, I decided to do my homework as soon as I came in after school, and that was easier for me than giving up my favorite show.

During Lent we attended the Way of the Cross service on Wednesdays, and during Holy Week we all take turns during the Vigil. We do not eat meat on Fridays, and we fast on Saturday. We go to confession so that we are worthy of communion on Easter Sunday.

All five Martini kids were in the choir, and there were numerous rehearsals before Easter. The Easter music is so spectacular and impressive, and we all are thrilled to be in this singing group with a choir director that we all love.

GG Francesca told us all about the huge parades and festivals in Italy at Easter.

There were candlelight parades, with statues of Jesus and Mary carried through the streets and much music and food available all over the town square. They always had Easter Pie made with lamb and eggs for their Easter meal. Delicious.

Here in America, we have our Easter Baskets which are filled with goodies by the Easter Bunny on Easter morning. We all go to church, even Dad, and then come home to our Easter dinner. Then we all go to watch bocci ball at Martini Park. The guys are so excited about the bocci ball, and it is fun to do this.

At the Catholic school at St. Joseph's, Father Salvatori took interest in me and encouraged me to become a priest.

I always had a funny feeling when I was with him, and I think he had an unhealthy interest in me. Years later, I found out that he had molested my sister Ginny, and I was horrified! I went through the act of going to church after that, but I will be happy when I move to New York and stop going to the Catholic church. I do not like hypocrites.

I love music, and I took piano and cello lessons growing up. I love all kinds of music and dance. My mother secretly took me to dance classes for years before she finally told Dad that I loved the classes. He got used to it, but I know he was disappointed in me. He has always wanted me to go out for sports and go hunting and fishing with him, but it is not my thing. I hope that sometime my father will be proud of me.

I have been in many dance troops and performances. I was Cavalier in Nutcracker at the Overture Theater. I think Mother and the girls were proud of me, but I don't think Dad was. One time my father called me a God-damn wimp, and I was crushed. He said Mother and the girls had spoiled me.

I have worked hard studying dance and ballet. I have worked hard in building up my body with exercise classes and weight building. I am six feet tall, and I have a lean, healthy physique—just perfect for dance. I think I am made for ballet.

I have a BS degree in dance and music from the University of Wisconsin, and I have loved every minute of it. Last summer, I went to New York for six weeks in the summer to study dance. These were the best weeks of my life because I was with other dancers who loved to dance as I do.

I have auditioned for the American Ballet Academy in New York City. I am so excited about this. I hope and pray that I will be accepted. My mother and sisters are all praying for me to get accepted. They do not want me to go so far away, but they all know how much this means to me. This is the most important thing in my life. I know dancers in New York, and they said they will help me find an apartment.

I just found out that I have been accepted!

I plan to tell everyone about my plans after Ginny's wedding. I hope my father doesn't make a scene.

My one-liner is, *"When the fog lifts in Los Angeles U.C.L.A."*

OLIVE'S STORY

I am the oldest daughter of Carmen and Gino Martini. I was born and raised in Greenbush, a part of Madison, Wisconsin.

Our neighborhood has always been the best neighborhood in Madison, where everyone knows everyone else and helps each other. We all get along—most of the time. We have a house on Regent Street quite near St. Joseph's Catholic Church and school. It is just like living in Italy, with everyone sticking up for each other. Do you want a job? Someone finds one for you. Do you want a house? Someone finds it for you and helps you move into it.

We all took piano lessons from the nuns, and later on, band. We sang in the church choir and in high school choir, but Michael was the one who really loved music and took dance lessons, including ballet. Dad did not know about the ballet lessons until one day Mother had to tell him that Michael was in a ballet performance at the Overture.

Michael was so excited to dance at the wonderful Overture, and we all went to the performance. He was so graceful, and he was an excellent dancer. Even Dad had to say that he was good.

After that, Dad never talked about Michael's dancing or studying dance and music at the University.

Michael earned a degree in music and dance and we were proud of him. Everyone loves Michael, and we loved that he worked hard to get his degree in spite of Dad.

The Bush is a small place, but there are a lot of businesses there and we are all involved in the church. Our father is in the Knights of Columbus, and our mother in the Altar Society. We are all involved in the school from K to 8th grade. For the most part, the nuns are pretty good teachers. They seem to favors girls, and we all wanted to become a nun at one time in our lives. None of us did. Father Salvatori tried to encourage Michael to become a priest, but he did not want that.

Our parents both worked long hours in the store, so our aunts took care of us during the day. We never had vacations, because the store was open every day except Sunday. My favorite aunt is Maria. She taught me how to sew and encouraged me to be a teacher. Maria taught high school English, and we all got help from her when we applied and interviewed for jobs. She also helped us write compositions when we applied at the university.

Maria is a collector of shoes and clothes, and she always looks like a model. I remember seeing her with huge rollers in her hair to produce beautiful waves. I teased her about the big rollers, but she taught me how to take care of my hair to make it look nice. We sewed beautiful clothes together.

Maria taught me how to sew, and I ended up being a Home Ec. teacher. I sew wedding dresses in the summers, and all of my sister's prom dresses. We had a whole closet of the dresses and we loaned them to friends.

When we were at Central High School Father Salvatori was very "friendly" with the girls. I always stayed clear of him because I thought he had a nasty look about him.

One day Mother asked Ginny to take some tomatoes from our garden to Dorothy at the parsonage. The housekeeper was gone, and Father invited Ginny in. He lured Ginny into the office, where he molested her, even though she fought to get away. Finally she got out of there, but Ginny will never forget the terrible scene.

Ginny came home and told us, and we were furious. We agreed that we would not tell Dad because he would have killed Father! We didn't go to the police or the bishop because in those days it was so embarrassing, and we just covered it up. None of us will ever forget it, and we warned all the girls in the school about him.

We all went to Central High School and we were very active. We were cheerleaders, active in forensics, debate (we all loved to argue), and I was Prom Queen. I sewed a luscious cherry-red dress with thin straps. Kinda daring, but mother said it was okay. I had a ball. We went to Turner Hall for dances and also to the Italian

Workman's Hall for dances. We also loved going to the movies. Mom and Dad talked about jitterbugging in high school and they loved the dances at Turner Hall too.

In our family we always have music. We play music in the store and at Martini

Boutique. We have gone through 78's, 33's and 45's, and we still have all the collections. At Christmas we played Mormon Tabernacle Choir music that is so inspiring and marvelous.

In the grocery store we played the 40's music mostly, which we all loved. We allhad our favorites, even though we said the music was "old-fashioned". We loved *Starlight, Brazil, Temptation,* and *Personality,* but we really got a kick out of the silly songs of the 40's: *Mairzy Doats, Cement Mixer, Chattanoogie Shoe Shine Boy, Pistol Packin' Mama, Managu-Nicaragua, Three Little Fishies, Minnie the Moocher,* and *I'm a Lonely little Petunia in an Onion Patch.* I liked *Sentimental Journey, String of Pearls, Inthe Mood,* and *American Patrol.* We played them at home and in the store. What fun!

My favorite uncle is Roberto, Mother's brother. He is married to Kathleen, and they have two boys, Andy and Noah, my cousins who taught me tennis and chess. They are so handsome, and I love them dearly. My friends do too!

Roberto is a family doctor and they have a big house in the Bush. His practice is on the first floor and apartment upstairs. We all have gone there with broken bones, poison ivy, sore throats, measles—you get the picture. He has always been so kind and has always helped us. He grew up in the Bush and now he has his medical practice here.

Roberto and Kathleen are environmentalists. They both work hard to make our environment clean and safe. Kathleen is a History teacher who has had many awards and accomplishments. I admire them both immensely.

My one-liner of the days is this: *"Acupuncture is a*

jab well done. That's the point of it.

In our family, our parents planted a tree when we had a baby in the family. My tree is an apple tree, which has wonderful apples growing on it every year. As i got older and my tree got bigger, I climbed its branches to "get away from it all." I felt so safe and happy in my tree, which I named AnnaMaria, Anna for short. I don't know where I got the name from, but it was fun to say. It was a great climbing tree.

Mother made apple pies, applesauce and apple butter from my apple tree, and I was always proud that the apples came from my tree. My job was to pick the apples in the fall. It always took a while because I love to spend time in my tree to just plain enjoy my tree and think. Anna was my thinking tree where I spent lots of time, just thinking. In the fall when my apple tree's leaves turned red, I would sit in the branches and feel the color in my body. What a delicious feeling.

Mother's sister Seraphine is very attractive, and she knows it. She has a standing appointment at the beauty shop for hair and nails and she buys her clothes at Yosts and Manchesters. The rest of us buy our clothes at Monkey Wards or sew them ourselves. Seraphine is sort of artificially perfect, and Mother is a stunning cutie-pie.

Quite a contrast. Seraphine has a job as manager at the prestigious Lorraine Hotel near the Capital Square. She says she has to look good to work there.

During the war, she was engaged to marry Paul, and we all loved him. He was from the Bush, and he loved Seraphine. She found someone "better" at her job and sent Paul a "Dear John" letter. We were all crushed, and worried about Paul. Seraphine and her husband still live in the Bush but we don't see much of her. She always says she's so busy, but Mother says, "She doesn't have chick or child, so why is she so busy?"

GG Francesca came over last night, and she is so funny. At 90 she gets words all mixed up. She said she went to the dermatologist because she had a spot that did not heal. She asked the doctor if she was going to do an autopsy on it. She always says, "What's so funny?" when we all laugh.

GG told us stories about when she was little. Her neighbor bought a wonderful farm machine that was an automatic chicken plucker. "Say that five times!" GG says.

We live in this huge beautiful house on the West Side now. I really miss the Bush, and I loved our old house on Regent Street. Thank God we all got to grow up in the Bush.

My brother Michael is graduating from he UW with a degree in dance and music. Michael has confided in me that he has auditioned at a ballet school in New York, and that he has been awarded a scholarship there. He is so excited about it. He wants to tell everyone after the wedding.

After high school, I went to UW and earned a degree in Home Ec. I got a teaching job in Madison at East High School and I just love it. I still sew wedding dresses in my spare time and summers, and love designing and sewing. We keep the closet full of formals that I have sewed for myself and my sisters.

I have had a few boyfriends, but I have always found something wrong with them. One had a yellow pickup.

Can you imagine that?

Now I think I have finally found the right man. His name is David, and he teaches science at East High School. He is so interesting and so much fun, and he's very handsome. I don't know if Dad will like him, because he is Jewish, and Dad wants all of us to marry Catholic men. Now that Ginny is marrying a Lutheran, maybe it will be better for all of us.

David's family lives in New York and they will probably want David to marry someone Jewish. We'll see how this all turns out. You never know how my father will react, but I know Mother will be fine.

Now we are getting ready for our family's first wedding, as Ginny and Erik are getting married in the summer. I wanted to design and sew Ginny's wedding gown, but I was overruled. I am making all the bridesmaid's dresses and it is so much fun. Ginny has chosen emerald green, and they will be beautiful, if I do say so! Erik's sister Margo will be in the wedding party with our three girls. So, I am making four dresses and one dress for the flower girl.

My one-liner is, *"Did you hear about the crossed-eyed teacher who lost her jobbecause she couldn't control her pupils?"*

BUBBLES STORY

I am the middle daughter of Carmen and Gino Martini. I am feisty and loud at times, and I always have fun wherever I go. I got my nickname from a Halloween costume that covered me all over with balloon bubbles when I was eight years old. The name stuck with me. My father said that Bubbles Martini is a good name, but my real name is Alayna.

I was born and raised in Greenbush, the best place in the city to grow up. My parents have a grocery store in the Bush that my grandparents had before us. As a child, I went there with my mother, and we all worked in the store when we grew up. We were taught to be very nice and polite to the customers, and it was hard with some people. Some were very demanding and insulting, but we were taught early on that this was our family's livelihood.

Our aunts helped to take care of us when we were little. Patrice was my favorite aunt because she always played games with us and had fun with us. She always baked delicious treats for us and taught us how to bake. Patrice's girls, Mandy, Carrie and Tara were like sisters to me and they are still my best friends. We still have sleep- overs all the time.

Patrice took us ice skating on the lake, and swimming in the summer at Brittingham Park. She taught us how to swim and skate, and we had such fun. Later, it was fun to go skating and swimming on our own as we got older. I loved it when a boy laced my skates and asked me to skate with him.

We all went to St. Joseph Catholic church and school. My cousins and all of us were together in the school, and sometimes we had a little too much fun and the nuns would call our parents. We took piano lessons from the nuns and Patrice had a piano for us to play. We all took turns practicing. The nuns would really scold us if we didn't.

I went to Central High School and met kids that were not Catholic. I was always told that kids other than Catholic were bad and I was not to have anything to do with them. What a surprise! I really liked them, boys and girls. We had so much fun with them in band, chorus, cheerleading, forensics, drama and lots of other activities. My friends from St. Joseph's school and all the rest got along just fine.

Our family Sundays were always so much fun. Our parents worked every day but Sunday, and we always had the same routine. Our father got up early to start breakfast, which we had at 10 o'clock. That way, Mother and we all could sleep in until then. I could always hear Dad singing this song as he cooked:

"Oh, it's good to get up in the morning when the sun begins to shine. It's four or five or six o'clock in the good old summertime.

And when the snow is snowing, and it's murky overhead,

Oh, it's good to get up in the morning, but I'd rather stay in my bed."

Then he chopped up onions, peppers, celery and olives and mixed them into an egg mixture. He added cut-up sausages and put the "Martini Egg Dish" into the oven.

On Saturdays at the store, Dad always bought dozens and dozens of sweet rolls from the bakery down the street, and on Sundays we had the ones that didn't sell. My favorite was, and still is elephant ears—that crispy flat sweet roll that is so delicious. If there were no more rolls from Saturday, Dad drove to the bakery and got some for our Sunday breakfast.

As he set the table, he sang goofy songs:

"It's hard to tell the depth of the well from the length of the handle on the pump." Repeat.

"There was a little elf-man down where the daisies grow.

I asked him why he was so small, and why he did not grow. He said he was as big for him as I was big for me."

"I never saw a purple cow, I never hope to see one.

But this I will tell you anyway, I'd rather see than be one."

After breakfast Mother and the kids got all dressed up and went to Mass. We'd always beg Dad to come with us. The nuns said he would go to straight to hell if he didn't go to church, and this was frightening to all of us. Dad would say, "I'll stay and clean up the kitchen. You go on to church." Looking back, I would have to say that our father loved all of us, and we had everything that we needed to make our lives happy. The nuns were wrong.

When we got home from Mass, the house always was clean and neat. Dad read the Sunday paper, and then we played games. In the summer Dad always played bocci ball with his buddies, and we went to cheer them on. Mother had a nice dinner at night after the games. Sometimes we went to movies. We all loved movies.

We never had vacations, but Sundays were our little "mini vacations."

I am so excited! Christmas is almost here, and I can hardly wait to see what presents I will get. The sisters at school tell us presents are not important, but to me they are. We should all pray and think about the really special role of Christmas, when Jesus was born.

I'm excited, too, because I can hardly wait to give Mother and Dad my present that I have made for them. I wove a basket that I think is really pretty, and it is my first one that I have woven. Sister Clemencia, our art teacher, taught us how to weave, and I love it. It could be used as a fruit basket or a sewing basket, or many other uses.

We have decorated our tree with popcorn and cranberry garlands, and pretty red ribbons. Of course, we have our beautiful angel on top. One of our relatives gave it to us for our tree. She brought it over from Italy.

Our radio has Christmas carols on all day long. We sing along with them and our whole family is cheerful and happy.

Our Sears Christmas catalog is full of marks and our names on our favorite things, and we all hope and pray that we get them. We all know that times are hard, so we don't mark too many things.

Mother has been baking cookies and making candy for weeks. She puts it into tins and locks it in a cabinet for Christmas. Last week I caught my brother unscrewing hinges on the cabinet doors and getting into the cookie and candy cabinet. He saw me and threatened to tell Mother that I had broken in. He gave me a cookie and candy, and then rearranged cookies and pieces of candy in the tin and screwed the hinges back into the cabinet. I feel sneaky about all this.

We got gifts from the Good Witch on Christmas Eve. We always had a great dinner, but no meat that night. We had sweet treats, baked pasta, and salted cod (baccala} with clam sauce, shared with dozens and dozens of relatives who came together for the dinner. Everyone brought some of the goodies we had. There was always music and the house was decorated with boughs, and of course the tree. GG said, "I love Christmas here, but I long for the traditions and my family in Italy."

On Christmas Eve, we go to church at six o'clock and the church is ablaze with lighted candles. Everyone has new clothes and we all feel so good about the Christmas season. In addition to the candles lit in the church, we all have a candle to light during the Mass. The music is amazing, and we all sing together. Our church organ plays impressive music that we all love.

When we get older, we go to Midnight Mass, which is a very special treat for us—sort of a rite of passage. We get sleepy, but we do our best to hide it. We kids are so happy that Dad goes to church at Christmas time.

Mother brings out our Christmas Book which we write in every year with a page for each of us. It's fun to read about former Christmases. We always moan and groan about writing in it—it's such a pain—but we always write, and it's always fun to read other's writings from year to year.

One year I wanted a nurse doll with a nurse kit

with crutches. It was expensive I knew, but I really wanted it. Mother and Dad agonized about this, and finally solved it. They bought a cheap doll and nurse kit, Mother sewed clothes for the doll, and Dad made a pair of crutches out of wood. They placed it in a nice box and I was in heaven. There it was in the Christmas Book.

I read on in the book and remembered that Sherry wanted a fuzzy pink robe and fuzzy pink bunny slippers. Of course, Mother sewed the robe and bought the bunny slippers.

As I read on I found GG Francesca had sewed nightgowns for us girls and pajamas for Michael with Christmas designs on the fabric. We all loved them every year.

GG tells us that in Italy many of the young people go skiing in the Italian Alps during the Christmas holiday. Sometimes there are bagpipers on the piazzas, and that was a lot of fun.

The end of the Christmas season is Epiphany Sunday on January 6 and we always take the tree down then, and all the decorations.

One year Mother bought dyed-to-match sweaters and she made skirts for us girls for Christmas, but when she started to wrap packages, she couldn't find the skirts. She looked and looked, and as it turned out, found them in June in a bag behind the shoes in her closet. We poor girls wore the sweaters without the skirts that winter.

As we girls got older, we brought our boyfriends to our Christmas parties. Mother always had a pair of men's gloves or a scarf to wrap for an unexpected boyfriend invited by one of us.

Looking back, we had so much fun at Christmas, and went to church a lot during this time. Church was a big part of our lives. We also spent a lot of time outside, sliding on the hills and skating on the lake. What a wonderful childhood we had.

We always went to church for New Year' Eve Mass. This was a night when even little kids could stay up until after midnight, and this was so much fun. Our mothers would always cook dishes and bake good sweets and take the food downstairs in the church before the Mass. Others cooked and got ready for the party right after Mass.

The church hired a band for dancing, and this was a good time for young people to learn how to dance. We all wore our best and prettiest clothes, and many romances started at the New Year's Eve party.

Everyone in our family loved to dance. The youngest of us practiced at home with our brothers and sisters. Many of the young girls danced together and hoped that some guy would ask them to dance. It took a lot of courage to ask a girl to dance, but Michael did most of the time. He was the best dancer in the hall, and everyone wanted to dance with him. He was nice enough to dance with his sisters!

If New Year's Eve fell on a Friday, there was always a special dispensation from the bishop so that we could all eat meat at the church.

In between dancing and listening to the music, we ate the delicious food and had coffee, tea, chocolate milk, or beer. Grammas held little babies and grampas danced with their grandchildren. All the families had little ones and old ones having a great time.

As the night wore on, little children grew sleepy and fell asleep on grandparents and parents' laps. We all listened to the music and visited with one another.

At 12 o'clock we had noise makers and hats, and everyone sang *Auld Sang Syne,* even the little ones. They were so tired, but they wanted to be part of the new year. Right after that, we all bundled up and walked home together in the beautiful snow. We slept late the next day and then watched the parades and the football games. What a fun holiday.

I had such good teachers at Central High School, and I always thought I would like to become a teacher. As it turned out, I went to UW School of Education and became a teacher of music. I am so happy that I have a job teaching at Georgia O'Keefe Middle School in Madison. What a great life I have. My best friends Kylie and Loxie also teach there and I am in heaven. We all exchange ideas and lesson plans. My boyfriend Patrick is a teacher here, too, and there's a big group of us that go to concerts, dinners, swimming and so forth. Life is good.

We are all aware that it takes years to become a good teacher and it's much easier if you have a good mentor. My mentor, Fiona, is so helpful, and I love her. I know that I can make a difference in the lives of my students when I teach them music and treat them with respect. If we have music in our lives we can do well in school and have a great life.

We have family stories of good and bad experiences in school:

Our father, Gino took a beautiful piece of curved wood with pretty, iridescent colors from their woodpile to school for show and tell in kindergarten. The teacher threw it in the waste basket and said it was dirty. Gino never took another thing to school for show and tell.

Mother and her friends in high school thought they were paying too much for movie tickets. Her English teacher suggested they write letters to the editors of the newspaper, and also make signs, and protest in front of the theater. They had fun doing this, and they got a student price for tickets.

My cousin was excited about some science experiments in middle school. He suggested that they put the experiment in the microwave to see if it would change the composition. The teacher laughed and made fun of him. I don't think he ever suggested anything again.

My uncle of 89 years old still talks about his high school band teacher who gave him private lessons on his trumpet and gave him solos in concerts. He said that was the highlight of his high school years. Dale went on to play in polka bands and later he was in the Army band during World War II. He always loved to play his trumpet. When Dale had Alzheimers he still remembered how to play Taps.

As a child, the father of a friend of mine went to a one-room schoolhouse in Little Falls, Minnesota. When he died at 102 years old, the family found a memory box with mementos of his life. One of them was an old, faded valentine given to him from his teacher in third grade years and years ago. Sigert had kept that valentine all those years through many moves in his life because he loved his teacher.

GG (my great-grandmother) had an eighth-grade teacher in Italy who gave her a part in a musical play at school. She said she never will forget how exciting that was.

My own love of reading grew out of teachers recommending books that were interesting to me and being nice to me. I think teachers have a responsibility to respect and listen to their students and to make them feel good about themselves.

Sometimes GG teaches me. When I talk about things I do (brag!) GG says, “Isn’t it grand to be perfect?” She has taught us that bragging is not nice, and we all have heard, “Isn’t it nice to be perfect?” many times.

GG and our whole family went down to State Street for lunch one sunny day, and when we got ready to order from the menu, GG said, “I’ll have the cream of asbestos soup, please.” We all laughed, and GG said, “What’s so funny?” The waitress went into the kitchen and I could hear them all laughing and giggling. GG is 90 years old, and she gets words mixed up in a fun and eccentric way and laughs along with us when this happens. We are all her little whippersnappers!

I have a new recipe for you that I just read in a magazine:

Elephant Stew:

1 sack flour

1 sack salt cooking oil 1 rabbit

1 elephant

Cut elephant into chunks and coat with flour and salt. Brown in hot oil. Place in large container and bake in medium hot oven for 48 hours. Serves 3800 people. If you expect a larger crowd, put in the rabbit. Don't do this unless it's necessary, as most people don't like hare in their stew.

My one-liner is, "*She had a photographic memory, but it was never fullydeveloped.*"

This story has a very dear teaching project that all teachers could use no matter the age of the student.

A VERY SPECIAL STORY. ALL GOOD THINGS...

He was in the first third grade class I taught at Saint Mary's School in Morris, Minnesota. All 34 of my students were dear to me, but Mark Eklund was one in a million. Very neat in appearance but had that happy-to-be-alive attitude that made even his occasional mischievousness delightful.

Mark talked incessantly. I had to remind him again and again that talking without permission was not acceptable. What impressed me so much, though, was his sincere response every time I had to correct him for misbehaving. "Thank you for correcting me, Sister!" I didn't know what to make of it at first, but before long I became accustomed to hearing it many times a day.

One morning my patience was growing thin when Mark talked once too often, and then I made a novice teacher's mistake. I looked at Mark and said, "If you say one more word, I am going to tape your mouth shut!" It wasn't ten seconds later when Chuck blurted out, "Mark is talking again."

I hadn't asked any of the students to help me watch Mark, but since I had stated the punishment in front of the class, I had to act on it. I remember the scene as if it had occurred this morning.

I walked to my desk, very deliberately opened my drawer and took out a roll of masking tape. Without saying a word, I proceeded to Mark's desk, tore off two pieces of tape and made a big X with them over his mouth. I then returned to the front of the room.

As I glanced at Mark to see how he was doing, he winked at me. That did it! I started laughing. The class cheered as I walked back to Mark's desk, removed the tape, and shrugged my shoulders. His first words were, "Thank you for correcting me, Sister."

At the end of the year, I was asked to teach junior-high math. The years flew by, and before I knew it Mark was in my classroom again. He was more handsome than ever and just as polite. Since he had to listen carefully to my instruction in the "new math" he did not talk as much in ninth grade as he had in third.

One Friday, things just didn't feel right. We had worked hard on a new concept all week, and I sensed that the students were frowning, frustrated with themselves, and edgy with one another. I had to stop this crankiness before it got out of hand. So I asked them to list the names of the other students in the room on two sheets of paper, leaving a space between each name. Then I told them to think of the nicest thing they could say about each of their classmates and write it down.

It took the remainder of the class period to finish their assignment, and as the students left the room, each one handed me the papers. Charlie smiled. Mark said, "Thank you for teaching me, Sister. Have a good weekend."

That Saturday, I wrote down the name of each student on a separate sheet of paper, and I listed what everyone else had said about that individual. On Monday

I gave each student his or her list. Before long, the entire class was smiling. "Really?" I heard whispered. "I never knew that meant anything to anyone." "I didn't know others liked me so much."

No one ever mentioned those papers in class again. I never knew if they discussed them after class or with their parents, but it didn't matter. The exercise had accomplished its purpose. The students were happy with themselves and one another again. The group of students moved on.

Several years later, after I returned from vacation, my parents met me at the airport. As we were driving home, Mother asked me the usual questions about the trip—the weather, my experiences in general. There was a lull in the conversation. Mother gave Dad a sideways glance and simply said, "Dad?"

My father cleared his throat he usually did before something important. "The Eklunds called last night, "he began.

"Really?" I said. I haven't heard from them in years. I wonder how Mark is."

Dad responded quietly. "Mark was killed in Vietnam," he said. "The funeral is tomorrow, and his parents would like it if you could attend." To this day I can still point to the exact spot on I-494 where Dad told me about Mark.

I had never seen a serviceman in a military coffin before. Mark looked so handsome, so mature. All I could think at that moment was Mark, I would give all the masking tape in the world if only you would talk to me.

The church was packed with Mark's friends.

Chuck's sister sang *The Battle Hymn of the Republic.* Why did it have to rain on the day of the funeral? It was difficult enough at the graveside. The pastor said the usual prayers, and the bugler played taps. One by one those who loved Mark took a last walk by the coffin and sprinkled it with holy water. I was the last one to bless the coffin.

As I stood there, one of the soldiers who acted as pallbearer came up to me. "Were you Mark's math teacher?" he asked. I nodded as I continued to stare at the coffin. "Mark talked about you a lot," he said.

After the funeral, most of Mark's former classmates headed to Chuck's farmhouse for lunch. Mark's mother and father were there, obviously waiting for me.

"We want to show you something," his father said, taking a wallet out of his pocket. "They found this on Mark when he was killed. We thought you might recognize it." Opening the billfold, he carefully removed two worn pieces of notebook paper that had obviously been taped, folded and refolded many times. I knew without looking that the papers were the ones on which I had listed all the good things each of Mark's classmates had said about him.

"Thank you so much for doing that," Mark's mother said. "As you can see, Mark treasured it."

Mark's classmates started to gather around us. Charlie smiled rather sheepishly and said, "I still have my list. It's in the top drawer of my desk at home."

Chuck's wife said, "Chuck asked me to put his in our wedding album." "I have mine too," Marilyn said. "It's in my diary"

Then Vicky, another classmate, reached into her pocketbook, took out her wallet and showed her worn and frazzled list to the group. “I carry this with me at all times,” Vicki said without battling an eyelash. “I think we all saved our lists.”

That’s when I finally sat down and cried. I cried for Mark and for all his friends who would never see him again.

Sister Helen P. Mrosla

This is a story that will have you crying when you get to the end.

LITTLE TEDDY STODDARD

There was a story many years ago of an elementary teacher. Her name was Mrs. Thompson. As she stood in front of her 5th grade class on the very first day of school, she told the children a lie.

Like most teachers, she looked at her students and said that she loved them all the same. But that was impossible, because sitting there in the front row, slumped in his seat, was a little boy named Teddy Stoddard.

Mrs. Thompson had watched Teddy the year before and noticed that he didn't play well with the other children, that his clothes were messy and that he constantly needed a bath. And Teddy could be unpleasant. It got to the point where Mrs.

Thompson would actually take delight in marking his papers with a broad red pen, making bold X's and then putting a big F at the top of his papers.

At the school where Mrs. Thompson taught, she was required to review each child's past records, and she put Teddy's off until last. However, when she reviewed his file, she was in for a surprise. Teddy's first grade teacher wrote: Teddy is a bright child with a ready laugh. He does his work neatly and has good manners...he is a joy to be around.

His second-grade teacher wrote: Teddy is an excellent student, well-liked by his classmates, but he is troubled because his mother has a terminal illness, and life at home must be a struggle.

His third-grade teacher wrote: His mother's death has been hard on him. He tries to do his best, but his father doesn't show much interest, and his home life will soon affect him if some steps aren't taken.

Teddy's fourth grade teacher wrote: Teddy is withdrawn and doesn't show much interest in school. He doesn't have many friends and sometimes sleeps in class.

By now Mrs. Thompson realized the problem and she was ashamed of herself. She felt even worse when her students brought her Christmas presents, wrapped in beautiful ribbons and bright paper, except for Teddy's. His present was clumsily wrapped in the heavy, brown paper he got from a grocery bag.

Mrs. Thomson took pains to open it in the middle of the other presents. Some of the children started to laugh when she found a rhinestone bracelet with some of the stones missing, and a bottle that was one quarter full of perfume. But she stifled the children's laughter when she exclaimed how pretty the bracelet was, putting it on, and dabbing some of the perfume on her wrist.

Teddy Stoddard stayed after school that day just long enough to say, "Mrs. Thompson, today you smelled just like my mom used to." After the children left she cried for at least an hour.

On that very day, she quit teaching reading writing and arithmetic. Instead she began to teach children. Mrs. Thompson paid particular attention to Teddy. As she Worked with him, his mind seemed to come alive. The more she encouraged him, the faster he responded.

By the end of the year, Teddy had become one of the smartest children in the class and, despite her lie that she would love all the children the same, Teddy became her teacher's pet.

A year later, she found a note under her door from Teddy, telling her that she was still the best teacher he ever had in his whole life. Six years went by before she got another note from Teddy. He then wrote that he had finished high school, third in his class, and she was still the best teacher he ever had in his whole life. Four years after that she got another letter, saying that while things had been tough at times, he'd stayed in school, had stuck with it, and would soon graduate from college with the highest of honors. He assured Mrs. Thompson that she was still the best and favorite teacher he ever had in his whole life.

Then four more years passed and yet another letter came. This time he explained that after he got his bachelor's degree, he decided to go a little further. The letter explained that she was still the best and favorite teacher he ever had. But now his name was a little longer. The letter was signed, Theodore F. Stoddard, M.D.

The story doesn't end there. You see, there was yet another letter that spring.

Teddy said he'd met his girl and was going to be married. He explained that his father had died a couple of years ago and he was wondering if Mrs. Thompson might agree to sit in the place at the wedding that was usually reserved for the mother of the groom.

Of course, Mrs. Thompson did. And guess what? She wore that bracelet, the one with several rhinestones missing. And she made sure she was wearing the perfume that Teddy remembered his mother wearing on their last Christmas together.

They hugged each other, and Dr. Stoddard whispered in Mrs. Thompson's ear, "Thank you Mrs. Thompson for believing in me. Thank you so much for making me feel important and showing me that I could make a difference."

`Mrs. Thompson, with tears in her eyes, whispered back. She said, "Teddy, you have it all wrong. You were the one who taught me that I could make a difference. I didn't know how to teach until I met you."

Elizabeth Silance Ballard

SHERRY'S STORY

I am the middle daughter of Carmen and Gino Martini, and we live in a large house in the Bush where everyone knows everyone. My parents work in their grocery store every day except Sunday, and our aunts take care of us during that time.

My favorite aunt is Bettina because she is so much fun and she spends so much time with us. Her children, my cousins, are just about my age, and we play a lot of games together. Celia, Mina and Amanda are just like sisters to me, and we get into mischief together.

Bettina is an excellent cook and baker, which probably led me to be a caterer later in my life. She taught me how to cook, and we tried new recipes that were good and fun to make. Sometimes we took dinner home, and my parents loved that!

Bettina told me a funny story about going to the Bahamas. On the plane on the way home, she was sitting next to a young woman who had surgery on the island because it was so much cheaper there than here. The surgery was to enhance her boobs and, on the plane, her artificial boobs exploded because of the pressure in the plane! Bettina felt so bad for the gal, but it was so funny. She had to swallow her laughs. I can just see her.

Growing up, we were all in sports except Michael.

He loved music and dance, but not sports. There were many anxious moments when Dad and Michael got into fights about sports. Dad wanted Michael to go hunting and fishing, but Michael did not like those things. The rest of us in the family hated these fights and thought Michael should be able to do what he loved to do.

I have always had many girl friends and I always went to the dances in high school, but not usually with someone I really liked. My sister Olive always sewed our formal dresses, and she is so talented. I once wanted a dramatic black dress for Prom, and we went shopping for fabric. We found the most beautiful black, silky fabric with embossed designs of flowers. It was the most elegant dress I have ever seen before or since. My sisters have all worn it, and we all still love it. A person feels really good when she is dressed in such an elegant dress.

One of my uncles, Vincent, worked for the Department of Natural Resources, and he became an expert on forest fires in the United States He was a member of the national training team for forest fires. He wrote training packages and taught many of them all over the country.

One of the training weeks, he went to Seattle, Washington and toured a training simulator in a submarine. It was so interesting, and he decided that the method could be used in forest fire training. He saw the same method used when he visited the Epcot Theme Park at Disney World in Florida. He was especially impressed by the depiction of Chinese landscape because it was so realistic. He wanted the forest fires used in training to be realistic like that.

He taught himself the method and developed the program (one of the first in the country). He bought multiple film projectors like the ones used at Disney World, and figured out how to use them. It was quite complicated, but he was determined to figure it out. He is very ambitious and aggressive, and the program was a huge success all over the country.

In the fire simulator, there are eight slide projectors and overhead projectors placed at intervals in the room, which project images of very realistic and frighteningly clear fires. A person at each projector operates and maneuvers the size and configuration of the fire, which is projected onto a large screen. A sound recorder records the crackling and popping sounds of the fire.

The fire overhead team appoints students to positions in the organization of fighting a large fire. The students think this is a piece of cake and that this will be an easy drill. As they get into it, they become worried and sometimes scared, and they begin to realize that this is serious business.

The fire boss is in charge of everything, with the following positions represented and appointed:

line boss

division boss

weather consultant

plane surveillance dispatcher

public relations

traffic control

equipment coordinator

food and medical water supply

publicity division boss

information official.

In some cases, the fire gets out of control and is a fire monster, very scary and realistic. The fire boss and the other positions must make decisions to get the fire under control and not lose the lives of the firefighters. They must also watch houses and buildings in the line of the fire and try to protect them. In the event of a crown fire, which is when the fire races to the crown of the trees and surges ahead, men and equipment must not be in the path of the fire.

Of course, the main objective is to save as much as they can of our valuable forest lands. Our forests are the breath of the land and are invaluable to the health and welfare of our world.

The lives of the firefighters is the number one priority. The U.S. Forest Service developed a fire-resistant fabric that was called Nomex, and Wisconsin provided jackets of this fabric to all the firefighters. They were bright yellow so that the firefighter could be easily seen and rescued if he were in trouble. Wisconsin also provided foil aluminum fire shelters that were folded into a rectangle and could be clipped onto his belt. They were trained to quickly unclip the shelter, put their hands and feet into the loops provided, lay on the ground covered with the shelter, and let the roaring fire, which generates its own wind, to thunder past them at lightning speed. The foil shelter is uncomfortable, but it saves lives when the unpredictable happens.

At the end of the exercise the students are exhausted and need a break. "Did you see a beautiful, nude girl during the exercise?" a student asked.

"I think I did. I was so involved in the fire, I thought I was seeing things that were not there!" was the reply.

Vincent told the students about the "Lady of the Mist" and all the students loved it. In the middle of a fire exercise, all of a sudden there was an image of a nude, beautiful woman with flowing hair and wispy, fluttery veils like mist all around her. She was just there for a moment, but all the foresters being trained saw her. She showed up in many presentations and became a kind of mascot for the group. The fire exercises were so real and so powerful that it was good to add a little pizazz to the fire training. He always ended a program with a beautiful sunset.

Vincent went to a meeting and gave his report for Wisconsin, and then said, "I'll give a report for Cal from Minnesota because he couldn't be here tonight." He took a tape recorder from his pocket and played the "report". It was many different loon calls. Everyone knows that Minnesota has a large population of loons, and everyone hooted with laughter, after which Vincent gave the real report from Minnesota.

His one-liner is, *"To write with a broken pencil is pointless."*

My friend Tasha and I both earned a Home Ec. degree from the UW, and we decided to start a catering business after university. I told Tasha that Bettina was the reason I took Home Ec.

Tasha spent a year working in the Oscar Mayer Wienermobile, traveling all over the country promoting Oscar Mayer products. It was a fun job, with TV appearances, newspaper interviews, grocery store functions, charity functions, marketing and sales. She and the others hired were brand ambassadors for Oscar Mayer and that started her on her path to food production. Tasha is very good at her job, and I was thrilled that she and I could start our business catering meals to people in Madison.

After I got my degree from UW, I knew I wanted to work in my mother's shop.

We had all worked in the shop growing up, but I really loved it. I hated to tell Tasha that I wanted to work full time in Martini Boutique, and I made the decision to do just that. Tasha was so gracious about it, and she already had a person to take my place. It was like she had known that I would do this! She said she knew I loved the business, but that I loved Martini Boutique better.

My mother and I went on buying trips to New York, which was very exciting. We expanded our line of clothing, and we had amazing jewelry, hats, homemade candy, many homemade knit and crochet items, and pottery. My Dad found incredible artists in Mexico, and our line of goods from there is really fantastic.

Now we live in a huge house in Middleton, far from the Bush that we love. Thank God we didn't move when we were all in school.

GG came rushing into our house one-day exclaiming, "What is the matter with me?" We all rushed over to see.

"As you know, I learned how to drive, and got my license, and I bought a nice little car that I just love—I never thought that I could be so independent and have so much fun. But I went to Vinny's garage to get some gas, and then drove around the block to drive through his car wash. Somehow or other I got the car crossways in the car wash! I got out of my car, but I got all wet from the water in there, so I honked the horn until Vinny came and opened the door.

"I felt so sorry for him, as he was nice about it, but quite flustered. He tried to drive the car onto the track, but he couldn't. In the end, he had to call two workers to unscrew the tracks and take them out, and then drive the car out. I am so embarrassed I could just crawl into a hole and die!"

My father said, "Oh GG, don't be so hard on yourself. I'll bet Vinny is telling everyone and laughing about it. I know Vinny, and he's a good guy. I think it's hilarious! This story will be all around the Bush by tonight."

"Vinny told me next time I need a car wash, he'll drive it in by himself," GG said.

GG came over again today, and she is excited because her letter to the editor was printed in the newspaper. She writes many letters to the editor but very few are printed. She came sweeping into the house with her walker and yelled the news. I am amazed at what she does at 90 years old. She exercises every single day and she walks for a total of one hour. Then at night, she does bed exercises. No wonder she can take care of herself.

I took GG to the dentist once and she had an hour of work done. She had one tooth extracted and one filled. When we went out to the car she said, "Thanks for taking me to the beauty shop!" That's the only advantage to getting old—forgetting everything.

GG, tell us a story" said Bubbles one time. We were all in a theater waiting to see a movie. We all silenced our cell phones, and GG says, "Oh my. I have my remote control for the TV in my purse instead of my cell phone! I'm such a ding bat. I wonder if I can silence the ads on the screen in this theater!" We all got a big laugh out of that.

"My good friend Shirley and I always forget words and names," GG says. "She helps me to remember a word or name and I try to help her too. Of course, she is a youngster, at only 84 years old. We're like Arsenic and Old Lace, except that we don't kill men with kindness!"

"What do you mean by that?" somebody bites.

"The movie Arsenic and Old Lace is funny, but really brutal if you know what I mean. Two little old sweet women have a boarding house with old men living there.

When one of the men has a disease or disability, and they both know he is in pain and will not get well again, the two old women give him homemade elderberry wine laced with arsenic. The victim dies painlessly, and Arsenic and Old Lace hide the body in the window box until another boarder comes and gets the body. This man has some mental problems, and he thinks he is a Teddy Roosevelt "Rough Rider," so he takes out the bad guys. You must get the movie and watch it!"

"It sounds like it's really fun! Ha Ha."

After the movie we walk to a restaurant, and GG says, "There are some dandelions that have gone to seed. Pick one and try to blow all the seeds off in one breath. If you do, you'll have a wish come true." Then she says, "The sun is so bright. Girls do not look right into the sun. It'll really hurt your eyes."

"How do you know that GG?" I ask.

"You know that I'm 90 years old. I have so much

in m head that it's busting. Lots of trivia that doesn't mean much," she says.

"I think you have some good ideas, but some of them are so entertaining. I love your stories.

"Do you girls remember Beatrice Dorietto?," GG asks. "I saw her mother in the store, and she said Beatrice got married last month. She said Beatrice's baby was born on time, but her marriage was late! Let's plan a baby shower for her."

"Tomorrow I'm going to my favorite mortician to have my hair cut." "What's so funny?

We were all sitting around the dinner table at home on a Sunday, having a great dinner of spaghetti and meatballs with a huge salad of greens and many different vegetables, and a desert that was out of this world.

"How nice to have a dinner with family. Just think, in a month or two Ginny will be married away from our home," Mother said. "This will be a sad and also happy time for me, because I want you to be happy, Ginny. Erik, it will be pleasant to have you in our family."

"I'm so happy to become one of your family. I want to thank all of you for welcoming me in your fantastic home. I think my family and your family will have many happy times together," Eric replied.

I said, "I have to tell you that the Martini Boutique is really going well. Customers love the Mexican pieces that Dad brought to us, and they are selling fast. Dad, you will have to make another trip down there soon."

"I didn't know Jose would have so many talented people in his little village," Gino said. "I was kinda worried that he was all talk and no substance. I'm relieved that he came through with the goods."

"And did you know that the thief who stole a calendar got twelve months?" "Oh, no. Another one-liner. Where do they all come from?"

"Well here's a pretty good story from surgery," says Erik. A brilliant surgeon that we all know and love got a call from his wife recently. Doc I-won't-mention-his-name was in surgery when his wife called on the OR phone. She asked if Doc was at a crucial part of surgery. I answered no, he was just closing up.

"Put me on speaker phone, please," she said. "Honey, did you notice anything strange when you drove out of the garage this morning?"

"No" he answered. "Why?"

"It seems that you drove the car through the garage wall last night, and when you drove it out this morning the whole garage collapsed. Did you notice that the garage collapsed when you drove out today?" she asked.

"Ahem...I must have been thinking of my morning cases," he mumbled, and then laughed hysterically with the rest of us.

My one-liner is, *"The guy who fell into an upholstery machine last week is nowfully recovered."*

Another one: *"Police were summoned to a daycare center where a three-year-old was resisting a rest."*

GINNY'S STORY

I am the daughter of Carmen and Gino Martini, and we all grew up in Greenbush, a part of Madison, Wisconsin. I'm so thankful that we grew up in the Bush, because now we live in a huge house on the west side of Madison. I love all our friends and family in the Bush.

My parents had a grocery store when I was growing up, and they had to spend a lot of time working there. Our aunts took care of us and we are so lucky to have spent all those days with our loving aunts and cousins.

My favorite aunt is Johanna. She is so funny and witty, and she understands when I have a problem. She always treated us like her own kids, with trips to the park, swimming, games and cards, ice cream and so many other fun things. I still go to visit her when I have time, and she's still wacky and interesting. I took my boyfriend Erik over to introduce her to him soon after I met him, and he liked her immediately. He saw our bond right away.

I have always had great friends and cousins, and my life has been fun and interesting. Mother has always encouraged us to try new things, and we have all taken her advice. I used to get a little angry when she urged us to try something new, and I didn't want to spend the energy on a new activity. It was a whole lot easier to just do the same old, same old.

We all went to St. Joseph's Catholic School from K through 8th grade. I had a terrible experience with Father Salvatori when I was in high school. We all expected priests, teachers and policemen to be helpful all the time. Father molested me in the parish office one morning when nobody was around. I will never get over it. It was so horrible, and I was hugely nauseated by his unspeakable behavior.

I was so ashamed, and I went home and told my mother and sisters. Did I egg him on? I wondered. Did I do something wrong? My mother told me that I had done nothing wrong, but Father had done the unthinkable. In those days we didn't report him to the police or church. I was so embarrassed, but I did warn my girlfriends about him. None of us told my father. I think he would have killed him.

After high school, I went to the University of Wisconsin and earned a B.S. in nursing. My fellow nurse and good friend, Willamina, who we called Mina, and I worked at the U.W. Hospital as surgical nurses for two years, and then decided to have an adventure and "see the world."

We were hired at Brigham and Woman's Hospital in Boston. What an adventure that was! There were Harvard docs everywhere, and the surgeries were sophisticated and complex, with many new procedures and new equipment. We thought U.W. Hospital was progressive and advanced, but we were experiencing very new technology here.

After a few years, Mina and I got homesick and we went back to U.W. Hospital in beautiful Madison, Wisconsin. I love it here, and we have fun doing things with our friends and families again. We are both happy to be home.

Mother has a great shop on State Street that she is so proud of. She is an amazing woman who is not afraid to start something new. Our family had the grocery store in the Bush, and when they sold it to my father's good friend, our family bought the store on State Street. The building had been for sale a long time, and it needed a lot of work to get it to where it is today. Mother said it was "tired and worn out."

They saw the potential of the store and they created an amazing and astonishing place with a lot of hard work. We all worked at it, but it was Mother and Sherry who did the innovative decorating of the store. They knew just what color to paint, and the unusual fixtures to buy. It really is a work of art itself, stocked with art pieces and handmade pieces of clothing. I am so proud of my family. Dad goes on shopping trips to Mexico to buy merchandise. It turns out he is a natural at doing this, and he loves it. He's so proud to buy these artistic pieces, that we all love. Who would have thought he'd do so well at this?

My boyfriend Erik and I walk down State Street often because it's my favorite place. We stop at Martini Boutique and say hello, then get a scone at Michelangelo's. Sometimes we eat food from the food carts, and sometimes we go to the Union on beautiful Lake Mendota and have their famous ice cream. We love to sit by the lake and watch the sailboats and play gin rummy at the iconic colored tables and chairs that the Union is famous for.

As we walk around the Capitol Square, I tell Erik

about the Raging Grannies group that GG and Mother are in. He had never heard of them. The Raging Grannies sing for peace, social justice, women's rights and conservation of our natural resources. They write lyrics to familiar songs and try to get their message across with humor. They wear bright colors and gaudy hats with political buttons on them, with shawls and aprons. The more outrageous the better.

The Raging Grannies sing at the Farmer's Market at the Capitol Square in the summers, and many other places. They always sing and march in the Willy Street Festival parade in September. The last few years GG has been wheeled in a wheelchair in the parade. She loves the parade but cannot walk it.

Another favorite place of ours to walk is Olbright Gardens, with their gorgeous flowering trees and flower arrangements and ponds. We love the Thai building that was donated by Thailand to Olbright Gardens. They sent it in many pieces and sent Thai workmen along to put it together here. It's a work of art. The rose garden is a special place for me too. In September we go to the Willy Street Festival.

"Don't you think this Willy Street Festival is fun, Erik?"

"There are certainly many odd-looking people here with odd-looking costumes," he said. "Madison is known for eclectic events, and here we are!'

"There's the Raging Grannies in the parade, right behind the Forward Marching Band," I said. "Look at those costumes. There's GG and Mother, all decked out in their Grannie Glam. The whimsical costumes and the fun and joy of the group is contagious and everyone around them sings along to their songs.

"Listen to their songs; *Corporations Are Persons Now, The Best Democracy Money can Buy, We Need Planned Parenthood, Radical Environmentalists, Black LivesMatter, If My Uterus Were a Gun, Standing in Need of a Single Payer, and Grannies Sing for Peace and Justice*. Grannies sing many songs about women's rights.

"They are singing their hearts out, and everyone is watching them and marching along. That's how it is when they sing at the Farmer's Market on Capitol Square

"I'm so proud of GG and Mother for being in a group like this. Sometimes it isn't easy. There are factions of people who get angry when they sing their liberal and progressive songs. They just ignore them and go on their way."

"I would love it if my mother joined the Grannies. She'd love it. I should talk to her about it. She's liberal, like me," Eric said.

"Look at the people on stilts," I said. "I don't know how they do it. There's a big group of them that go to parades and put on demonstrations. The costumes are outrageous and creative. And there's the giant bubble machine in that huge antique convertible, with Uncle Sam driving it!"

"I like the unicycles. That takes a lot of practice to learn to ride one of those. I don't think I could ever do that."

"Let's get some of that wonderful Mexican food at that stand. I love enchiladas, but I love quesadillas too. Which do you like?"

"Actually, I love BBQ chicken calzones and porta-bella penne at the Italian stand.

I can't decide what to get!"

"Guess you can get your Italian and I'll get my Mexican. I'll meet you here at the tables."

After the parade, GG and Mother join us at the table and have lunch with us.

Mother had Thai food and GG had Italian.

"Ipsy Dipsy Doodle," said GG. "I'm trying to remember what I was going to look for here at the Willy Street Festival. What was it? I'm getting so wacky. I forget what I remembered!"

Here's a one-liner. "*When she saw her first strands of gray hair, she thoughtshe'd dye.*"

"I'm reading a book about anti-gravity and I just can't put it down."

day."

"Let's go to dinner tonight at a special place, just you and I," said Eric. "What's the occasion?" I asked.

"I have something that I want to talk over with you."

"I love to go to Bunky's Restaurant. Is that special enough for you?"

"Sounds good to me. First, let's take a walk to Picnic Point. It's such a beautifulThe walk was so nice, with Lake Mendota making the walkway magical. We were all alone there, and the birds were singling just for us!

Erik got down on one knee and asked me to marry him. He took a small square box out of his pocket and took out a stunning ring.

"What do you say, darling? Can I put this ring on your finger?"

"Erik, I am so happy! Yes, yes, yes! I'll never forget this day. I can't wait to tell my family and friends. They will be so happy."

"What the heck! Let's call both of our families and tell them to meet us at Bunky's and we'll tell them all together. Is that okay with you, Ginny?"

"That is perfect! Let's make it a party," And what an exciting party it was. Both families came and it was so fun to talk about the wedding coming up. We will have a great life.

But my father does not seem excited. He told me that Erik is not good enough for me. I am worried that he will not approve the wedding, and it makes me so sad. It's like he is with Michael, with his disapproval of Michaels's dance and music. Now I know how Michael feels.

Plans for the wedding now dominate our lives. My father is building an in-ground swimming pool in our yard just in time for the reception here. I think Dad wants to impress Erik's parents. Mother does not want this, but he is doing it anyway. Maybe we should just run off and elope!

My latest one-liner is, *"With her marriage, she got a new name and a dress."*

One day Erik and I were walking down State Street toward the Student Union and were talking about how we decided to go into our medical careers.

"I always knew I would become a surgeon," said Erik. "My father and my grandfather took me to observe surgery from when I was little. I think they were grooming me to go into the profession. But—I loved it! I can't think of another profession that I could be in. Every case is different and I hope and pray that I am doing something good for humanity. That's really important to me."

"Did you ever have uncertain feelings about your course of study?" I asked. "No," Erik said. "I'm so lucky that I was able to do what I wanted to do. My brother Nick always wanted to be a teacher, and I'm happy that he did follow up on it. My father never should have made him feel guilty about not becoming a doctor. I feel badly for him. I am so proud of him because he is an excellent teacher, doing what he wants to do. What about you, Ginny?"

" I can honestly say that I am doing what I want to do and what I am destined to do," I replied. "When I started school in nursing, I didn't know what part of nursing I would end up in. There are so many different jobs in nursing. I shadowed a surgical nurse for a week, and I was hooked. I was worried that the "blood and guts" would bother me, but I was mesmerized with the intricate surgical experiences. I knew right away that this is what I will do the rest of my life. The anatomy of the human body is intriguing. I simply love my work."

"The other side of the story is the depressing feelings when you lose a patient in surgery," Erick said. "Have I done absolutely everything that I could do to cure this patient? I have seen my father and grandfather come home so sad and upset. We all knew we would have to be quiet and kind to them when this happened. As a nurse, my mother knew just how to handle the situation and help my father. I think you will be just like her when I need you. The torment when that happens is so severe.

Heaven knows that I will need you then."

"Eric, you forget that I will need moral support as well as you do, because I will experience the same failures in surgery. I know that all surgeries do not turn out the way we want. I think we will be good for each other in our careers and private lives. We are good for each other now."

"I'm so glad that I have found you," Erik said. "We were meant for each other.

We think alike and love the same things."

"Okay", I said. "Now I will beat you in Gin rummy!"

"Oh, no you don't. I feel lucky today. I guess it's because I beat you last weekend. I can do it again."

We were walking around the Capitol Square another time, and I said, "There's a Bucky Badger in front of the Park Inn. They bought it this year and it is a great Bucky, painted by a local artist. There were 85 Buckies made of fiberglass, each six feet tall and weighing 120 pounds. Building, painting and selling them was a successful event that benefitted cancer, and the University Sports Commission.

"A couple of years ago there was a similar event where they had 100 cows made of fiberglass. They were life-size and quite impressive. The Brat House on State Street has one with a shelf where you can put your drinks on their patio. It's a pretty unique place.

"I remember some of the cows—each one was a work of art! My dentist bought one and has it on the lawn by his building. They were all sold, and the proceeds went to various charities. Good project.

"Madison has some unusual, snazzy flash happenings that are so much fun. I loved living in Boston, but Madison is so much more fun. Of course, meeting you, Erik, is the best thing that has happened to me!"

"Oh, Ginny, I love hearing you say that. I am so delighted that we have found each other. What a life we have!" Eric declares.

"Lets talk now about religion in our marriage," I said. I told you that Father Salvatori molested me when I was in high school. It's very hard for me to talk about. Since that terrible event, I have hated to go to the Catholic Church. My father would not like that, but it is true. I have decided that I would like to go to your Lutheran Church and see if I feel comfortable going there. I would love to have one religion in our family, just as your family and mine have had. Church has always meant a lot to me."

"I can just imagine how hard this is for you to talk about, Ginny. Please know that we can talk about everything and anything, and I know that it will make us closer and more confident in our marriage. You know that I would love it if you decide to come to our church, and my family would love it too. But it must be your decision. It's a big step," Eric said.

I went on, "I think about priests in my church molesting children, and it turns my stomach. I remember seeing Father Salvatori looking at Michael in a strange way. How many children did he molest? The Catholic Church is very wrong in their belief that priests should not marry. Their lives are not normal, and they cannot understand the ups and downs of a normal family. How do they counsel a family without knowing how a normal family works? Most men need a wife and family in their life. That's the nature of the beast!"

"Let's plan to go to my church once in a while, whenever you feel comfortable about it, and take it from there," Eric said. "We can make an appointment to meet with our minister, Rev. Nelson, when you think you want to. My darling, I hope we can work this out."

Eric and I invited all of our families to the Essen Haus for a German dinner tonight.

"Oh no! Sauerkraut and dumplings! I like Italian food better," my father complained.

"Now Gino, give it a chance. It's so nice of them to invite us," Mother said. "I'd rather go to our friend's restaurant and have Italian, dang it."

"This is our family, Gino. Grin and bear it!" "All right. What should I wear?"

"Just a nice shirt and pants. It's not formal."

When we get to the restaurant, he asks Erik's father, "What do you recommend we order here, Sean?"

"I love the sauerbraten veal dish here," Sean said. "It's a great favorite of mine." "I love the spatzle with sauerkraut more than anything," Erik's mother, Lydia says.

"I'm a little bit confused with the menu," Father admits. "Kartoffelpuffer, rinderroulade, schweinshaxe, kartoffelk loesse, and bratwurst. I thought Italian dishes were confusing. The only one I have heard of is bratwurst, but I think I will order the sauerbraten because you recommended it, Sean."

"Good choice, Gino. I think you will love it."

"Heh, this is really good," Father says. "who would have thought I would like German food! I think I will come here often. Anyone else who would like to come with me? I have passed this restaurant so many times, and thought nothing of it and the food. I have really missed this one. It's an old German restaurant, isn't it?"

"I think it's the only really good German food in the city. We come here for special occasions."

"I have a funny story about high school activities," says Eric's brother Nick, changing the subject. "An English teacher named Zona proof-read and approved an article for the school newspaper. The article was well-written, about a science project, and Zona complimented the student on it. The last line in the article was a number to call for more information about the science project, but the telephone number turned out to be a porn number! Zona had to go to the school board for a hearing on this one. It was not her fault, the board decided."

"There are so many caring teachers that I know," says Bubbles. "I know a high school teacher who helped many of her students on the road to University. Isobelle was a forensics and debate coach, so she was able to get to know these students well because they all spent so much time together.

One student, Jane, was a very smart, cute girl with a lively personality, who was being raised by a single mother. Isobelle helped Jane apply for University and helped her with a narrative. She was accepted. Isobelle drove Jane and her mother to the U and helped her get settled in her dorm. In my opinion, these teachers are my heroes."

Eric's family, the Schwantes, and the Martini family get together at our beautiful home in Middleton. Everyone knows that my father won the house in a poker game, and the Schwantes are very curious about that. I think everyone is curious about that!

I still have the feeling that my father does not like Erik, and I do not like that attitude. Erik is very successful and a great guy. The important thing is that I adore him and he adores me. That's all that is important.

Erik and I talk about going to marriage counseling with Father Danny. We both like him so much and are getting a lot of good out of his counseling. Father Danny is such a good friend to the family.

Wedding plans are also talked about with the Friday night rehearsal dinner being at the Nakoma Country Club, the wedding at St. Joseph's Church, and the reception at the Martini home. Father Danny and Rev. Nelson will both officiate at the wedding.

The question of communion came up, and Father Danny said that only Catholics can receive communion. Rev. Nelson said that everyone can receive communion in his church. They settled it with Father Danny giving communion on the right side of the altar, and Rev. Nelson giving it on the left side of the altar.

Olive wanted to make my wedding gown, but I said that it was enough for Olive to make the four bridesmaids dresses and the flower girl's dress. We have decided on emerald green for the dresses, and Olive is excited and can't wait to start sewing. What a trooper!

Everyone gets together to hunt for the dress. My father insists that he go along because—as he says— "I'm paying for it. I want to help pick it out!"

It is a disaster! Father loves a horrible, ruffly wedding gown and he wants to buy it for me. We go home in a huff.

A few days later we all go without him and have a wonderful time looking for the perfect gown. I chose a gorgeous gown and even Olive loved it. Lydia and Eric's sister Margo Schwantes came, too, and they had a perfectly marvelous time.

We also shopped for and found lovely emerald green

fabric for the bridesmaid dresses for Olive Bubbles, Sherry, Margo and the little flower girl, Jordan. Olive can't wait to start sewing.

My father wants to impress the Schwantes, so he called a building contractor about building a swimming pool in his yard for the reception. The builder said he couldn't guarantee that the pool could be finished in time for the wedding, but my father insisted that they start to dig. My mother was nervous about this, but father said, "Don't worry. It will be finished in time for the wedding. There's a perfect spot in the yard for a swimming pool."

ERIK'S STORY

I am the oldest child of Sean and Lydia Schwantes. My father and my grandfather are both surgeons at U.W. Hospital in Madison, Wisconsin, where I am also a surgeon. Three generations of surgeons at U.W. Hospital is a really special thing for our family. I am honored.

I grew up in a nice neighborhood in Middleton, where we had strong family friends. We always had kids from the neighborhood in our house and yard, playing games and having fun. My mother is a nurse, but she was a stay-at-home mom after we came into the picture. Our lives are so full of good times growing up and we are thankful.

A big part of our lives is our church. Bethel Lutheran Church is a caring and thriving church with many activities for young and old. We grew up being a part of so many programs, all interesting. There is so much music in the church and we were all in the choirs, Sunday Schools, work camps in the summers, and some were just plain fun activities.

I went to Madison Preparatory School (Mad Prep) from K through high school and I have good ties to fellow students there. We had to study hard because the standards were high. It was a good background for medical school.

I love my profession. Every day is so fascinating, and every patient is different and challenging. What could be better than that?

I am engaged to an intelligent woman, Julia, who is a professor of Early European History at UW. She is quietly elegant and interesting. She goes to Europe often with students and without students. Europe is her main topic of interest.

Lately in the staff OR lounge I have been noticing a new surgical nurse, who is a master at storytelling. Here she is, telling one in the lounge.

"This is a story about an arrogant surgeon at Brigham and Women's Hospital. The chief cardiac surgeon, who was near God-like to all the staff, was quite an ass. Once, while I was scrubbed in a CABG with him, a visiting Chinese medical student was observing. He was looking over the anesthesia screen while the surgeon was telling him the steps of the procedure. We had just opened the chest and the heart was not yet on bypass, and down comes a pair of wire-rimmed glasses on top of the beating heart. With every heartbeat the dirty wire-rimmed glasses bounced up and down on the heart.

"You could hear a gasp from all of us at the same time as we saw this. The surgeon picked up the glasses from the heart and threw them across the room, hitting the OR wall and falling to the floor. He then looked up at the medical student and said, "Why don't you just lean over and take a shit on the heart, for Christ's sake?" You could visibly see the color leave the student's face as he felt his way out of the OR.

"Doc changed his gloves, irrigated the heart over

and over and gave antibiotics.

I can still see that heart with glasses going up and down, up and down!"

Everyone began to laugh, and I wondered about the delightful nurse who told the story.

Later on, we were all drinking coffee and relaxing in the staff OR lounge between surgeries and I asked my friend Max who she was. Max said, "She's Ginny Martini, and she's the new nurse on Doc Sophie's neural surgical team. She's smart, stunning and a great nurse."

"Do they call her Gin Martini? That's hilarious!" I said. "She must be pretty good if Sophie invited her on her team. She's pretty particular about who she adds to her team. I haven't seen Ginny around. Is she new here?"

"She just came home to Madison this year. She had been working at Brigham and Women's Hospital in Boston and she has some very interesting experiences to tell."

My God, she is beautiful! Max is dating her and I know he likes her. He tells me that Ginny loves the Badger football games and all the Badger sports. She also loves the symphony at the Overture. I can't imagine Julia going to a football game! I have to be careful here. I'm thinking of Ginny too often.

What the Hell. I have an extra ticket for the Badger game Saturday afternoon, and I think I will ask Ginny if she would like to go. Julia hates football and she wouldn't care if I went with Ginny.

Ginny said yes, but rather reluctantly, I thought. She probably was thinking about what Max would think. I don't think they are engaged.

Ginny has pizazz! I picked her up and she had Badger clothes on and she looked like a million dollars. She knows all the Badger's names and she loves the cheers and band. I do too! She talked about Max and I talked about Julia and we had a great time. We went out to dinner afterwards and talked about everything and everybody. The evening went too fast, and we were saying goodbye. I hope we can to this again.

Ginny told a funny story in the cafeteria yesterday.

"A man comes into surgery and he says he has an obstruction in his penis. Doc says, 'Let's see what it is.'

The guy says, 'Oh, I know what it is. It's a birthday candle.' 'How did it get in your penis?'

'Well, it was my girlfriend's birthday, and I told her to turn around for a big surprise. I took off my pants and put the candle in my penis and lit it. Then I told her to turn around, and I sang Happy Birthday to her. She laughed and laughed. Then I blew it out and tried to take the candle out. I couldn't get the damn thing out! That's my story."

I can't imagine Julia telling a story like that! We all thought it was hilarious.

I have been thinking of telling Julia that we do not have the same interests and that we should date other people. Out of the blue, Julia called me and met for coffee. She told me that she was going to Europe with a group from the U and she was

especially interested in one of the profs going on the trip. She said she is very fond of him, which means to me that she loves him.

Julia told me that we just did not have the same interests, but that she liked me and hoped that we could still be friends. She then gave me the little square box with the engagement ring in it. I guess I mumbled a few words about how I would miss her, and then I left. I have a bruised ego, but I think I will get over it. Now, I must worry about my friend Max, who I went to medical school with. He's a great guy, and I don't want to hurt him.

Next week, I call Ginny to invite her to the symphony at the Overture. She loves the symphony and says yes. I know she is agonizing about Max, but Ginny tells me that she has talked to Max and it is over. I'm sorry for Max, but I'm happy for me. That's really terrible of me. We both love the same things. I think I am in love.

Our family has Ginny over for dinner, and she is nervous because she knows that our family loved Julia. Everyone is really nice to her, and she likes them all. Nick and my sister Margo love her stories. My father and mother love to talk about experiences in the hospital with Ginny and me.

My father told a good story about a medical experience. "During an above-the

-knee amputation at a large trauma center, the vascular surgeon was quite a witty guy. It was customary for an orderly to be called to the OR to pick up large specimens.

There was quite a turnaround in orderlies at the time. We just made the last cut and were waiting to hand off the leg, so an orderly came in to help.

"The surgeon handed the leg to the orderly and said, 'Shake a leg, buddy.' The orderly fainted on the spot with the amputated leg landing on top of him. He left and never came back. We found out it was his first day in the OR. The surgeon called him to apologize, but to no avail."

Ginny told the story about Surgeon Rosie. "I knew a brilliant surgeon at Brigham and Women's who was so fat that he had trouble finding scrubs to fit him. He entered the surgical area one day in a woman's scrub dress with his hairy legs showing. We all giggled, and he said, "I couldn't find a big enough scrub, so I had to wear this. Don't tell anyone and please do not take my picture." His nickname was Rosie after that.

My mother was laughing so hard at the stories. Then she told a story. "A young girl came into the OR with what we thought was a stomach tumor. She could not eat and had stomach pain. Her CT showed a large mass filling her entire stomach. We opened and explored her abdomen only to find her entire stomach filled with a human hair ball. After recuperating from surgery, she was fine. Her mother told us that her daughter sucked on her long hair at night. Her hair was cut the next. day."

"My God, I have to tell a story, too," I said. "I can't let all of you show me up! There was a nurse who seemed to fall asleep at every event. She was circulating a TPPV delicate laser eye procedure where the room is kept dark and quiet. We were all tense, and the nurse got up in the dark room and landed with one foot in a rolling kick bucket used for throw-away sponges. She flew across the OR like a professional skateboarder, and the bucket rattled and made quite a racket. '#%$^&*@!,' said the doc."

"I can't remember when I have had such a good time and laughed so much," said my mother.

Margo said, "I can't wait to become a nurse and have these experiences!"

Nick said, "We don't have that much fun teaching school, but someday I will tell you all stories about teaching kids!"

I am so happy. I think that this is the very first time I have been in love. I have not told Ginny that I love her. Sometime in the near future, I am going to ask Ginny to be my wife.

I am worried about my sister Margo, though. She and I were so close, and now she doesn't talk to me. I think she's in with a group of students and she is not doing well in school. I'm going to ask Ginny to include her in some of our fun adventures.

We are now dating every week, and the two families think of us as a couple. We seem to have fun everywhere. Things seem to be going well with Max, too, and he and his date frequently double date with Ginny and me. We are so happy that it turned out like this!

Ginny and I were driving to a movie, when she said "Erik, will you stop and get a bottle of water for me? I'm so thirsty."

"Sure. I'll stop at this drug store." I got out and came back with the bottle of water. Ginny had locked the car door and was putting on lipstick and powdering her nose.

"Hey, Ginny, let me in!" She grins. "What? I can't hear you."

"Ginny, let me in!" Finally, she unlocks the car door and I get into the car. "What's the deal? You crazy kid! I don't know what you are going to do next! I

love it!"

"You have just passed a test," Ginny says. "I do this to anyone I date to see what his reaction is. If you had been mad and grumpy, I would have nothing more to do with you. That would have been the end of our relationship."

"Well, I'm glad I passed the test. How many other tests are there?"

"You will have to wait and see! Now, on to the movie. I love a man with a good sense of humor."

After the movie Ginny says, "Erik, what do you think of Governor Walker?"

"I think he is a jerk and is ruining Wisconsin. He has cut budgets on stem cell research and other vital research at the U.W. and has cut budgets for the University and public schools. What he has done to teachers with Act 10 and abolishing collective bargaining is deplorable.

He favors tax cuts for the wealthy and thinks it will "trickle down" to the masses.

What a lot of hogwash! He's just like Reagan and Tricky Dick. I could go on and on about what Governor Walker has done to all of us, but I think should stop. What do you think of Governor Walker?"

"I agree with everything that you said, and I love you! You have just passed another test, Erik."

Here's my latest one-liners. *"When you get a bladder infection, urine trouble."* *"When chemists die, they barium."* I couldn't resist throwing them in.

It's a beautiful day in Madison, and it's great to be alive and walking down State Street.

Ginny says, "Let's walk over to Bascom Hall and rub Lincoln's foot for luck in planning our wedding. I always rubbed his foot before every exam that I took all through my years at the UW. I love this statue of Abe. At graduation, everyone climbs a step ladder so they can rub Lincoln's nose for good luck in finding a good job.

Somebody told me that this is the only replica of the original statue, which is cited near Lincoln's birthplace in Hodgenville, Kentucky."

"Here's another story about Bascom Hall," I said. "Jim Mallon and Leon Varjian ran for student council at UW many years ago, and they were both pranksters. They ran for the fun of it as Pail and Shovel candidates. Their big promise was to bring the Statue of Liberty to the campus if they won.

"They did win—there were no other candidates in the race—and they did indeed bring the Statue of Liberty to the campus, on Lake Mendota behind the Student Union. Everyone in Madison came to see the statue of Liberty on the ice in dead winter. Of course, the statue had sunk into the ice and the upper part of it was the only part that could be seen! It appeared she had been dropped into the lake.

"The other thing that Jim and Leon did was to put plastic pink flamingos on the area around Bascom Hall. Dozens and dozens of them graced the impressive Bascom Hall to everyone's astonishment. Where did they come from?

"Many years later, Doug Moe, a Madison Newspaper writer, wrote about the pink plastic flamingos in an article. Alder Marsha Rummel read the article and proposed to make the flamingos the official Madison bird. City Hall council members voted, and the plastic pink flamingo is now the official Madison bird. Madison is known for its liberal and nonconventional, progressive charm and charisma."

All of us were in the staff OR Lounge after a stressful day of surgery.

"I have a story that is so bizarre that you will not believe it!" I said. "A friend of mine told me that he had patients with severe breathing problems. Harvey and his son, Harvey Jr. were told by a doc somewhere in the east to smoke cigarettes three times a day to clear the bronchial tubes and make you breathe easier. Can you imagine a doc telling you that?"

Everybody chimed in; "Does he live in the Dark Ages?" "Cigarette companies would love that!" "You're right, Eric. That is really bizarre."

"Ginny said, "Here is a story that a member of a rescue squad told me about one of his calls, in Jake's own words. These people are all volunteers and they put in a lot of time in training and calls in their communities."

Oh, no. The phone is ringing and it's 2 a.m. I know it's a rescue squad call, but I'd love to hunker down and ignore it. I have to answer it.

"Hello? I said. "What do you have? Oh, no—a head-on two-car crash! How does it look?"

"Pretty bad. We have to take both ambulances, and I've called Joe and Al. We have to hurry. Get your butt over here."

The scene is pretty bad, as the caller said. The sheriff department was using the jaws of life to get one of the victims out of the car. He seemed out of it and was not responding.

"If you can find out their names, write it on their foreheads so when docs get them they can use their names," we are instructed

Al and I splint bones, give oxygen to those who need it, and clean up wounds. Then we call the hospital to give information on the patients and drive to the hospital. They need time to get ready for four serious patients.

We are volunteers for our small-town rescue squad, and we do the best we can on these calls. Our little town is 35 miles from a hospital or clinic, and that is why we have organized and trained our volunteers. We have had many fund raisers to buy the ambulances (second-hand) and equipment. The whole town is involved in this endeavor. I hope our patients make it to the hospital.

When we get there, the hospital staff is waiting at the doors. They take the four patients in, and there is a rushed feeling of urgency as the docs and nurses judge which are the most critical. Joe and I help load and unload the wounded and talk to the docs about what happened.

Joe tells me, "We were right about how bad Jim is. I heard the doc say that they have to do a trigonometry on his throat so he can breathe!" Everyone heard this and we all cracked up. Joe laughed too, when we hold him what they were going to do.

After that, everyone seemed more relaxed and calm, and we all had a good laugh about it.

Another time we were in the OR lounge again. "Boy, this has been a tough day, with multiple cases and many things that have gone wrong," I said. "What in hell was wrong with Doc. Ben today?"

"Ben has his favorite rectal speculums flown in from somewhere in the UK. He bought them himself, and they are sterilized only for his own use. Today they needed to be used multiple times in a row, and the surgical tech decided to autoclave them. They came out as a melted ball of rubber/plastic mess. Sheepishly, the tech brought them to the surgeon, and he said "*&%$@#! They are not really rectal worthy now, are they!"

"So that's what happened!" I said. "Surgeons have their favorite instruments. I knew one who did not want any other surgeon to use his own personal instruments, so he had the handles of all of them dipped in gold. There were two pans of instruments that were labeled just for him. He had quite a meltdown if they were not opened for each of his cases. Once they were not there for his surgery and he pushed the charge nurse against the wall and hit her. He lost his OR privileges for six months because of this, and everyone agreed that he had it coming."

"Even surgeons who are famous can get into trouble, I guess," said Ginny. "I'm glad I wasn't that nurse who was pushed against the wall."

"It's common for surgeons to nickname instruments" I said. "Some stick, and become a facility named instrument. One was a large aortic clamp that was named by a vascular surgeon. He had forgotten the name of this clamp once when he needed it and asked for the "umm-umm, give me the Goat Crusher." Forever more that clamp was referred to as such.

"Now I can't wait to get home, have a nice hot shower and relax. A good dinner would help, too. I'm not going to think of instruments or surgery until morning!"

Bubbles, Nick, Ginny and I walked down State Street one day and stopped for a coffee at Michelangelo's.

Bubbles was gruff and snappy, not at all like she usually is.

"All right, Alayna. What's going on with you?" said Nick.

"I'm so angry I could rip someone's head off! You know the bully that I told you about? He's still going after little Peter, the adopted kid of such nice people. He told Peter to go back to Mexico. Peter said, 'I'm not from Mexico. I'm from Bolivia.'

'Well, go back to Bolivia, then.' I heard the bully mutter, 'Now I know why his mother gave him away!'

"Peter looked like he would cry, and I took him into my office. He said, 'I don't know why he hates me so. I really try to stay away from him and not look him in the eye. I go out of my way to avoid him, but he always seems to find me. I don't know what to do.'

"I talked to him as long as I had time for, and then went to find Bernard, my good friend who is a counselor. We talked about it and arranged to have the bully's parents and our principal have a conference with us. I just don't know how to stop this sort of thing. Should the police be called about this? I have seen bullying in our school so often, and it follows the victim home on the internet. I have seen parents take their child out of our school and enroll him/her in another school because they could not stop the bullying. I am so frustrated!"

"Alayna, I know what you are going through. I have seen it on the high school level. It makes me so angry, and I have tried to find a way to help these kids. One time a note was found that the bully was going to kill the victim, and we had to call the police and the parents. The parents both said, 'He didn't mean it. What's the big deal?' This is what we're getting from the parents We're hitting a brick wall."

"I'm trying to think of how to help these poor kids," Alayna went on. "I wonder if the principal, counselors, athletic coaches and teachers all got together and worked out a plan to engage popular sports stars to support students who are bullied and give them advice. If popular sports kids stand up to bullies, I think the bullies would back off. This would have to be followed up so that there is no more cyber bullying. It's worth a try."

"This is the reason some teachers quit teaching and find another career. It wears you down," said Nick.

"Okay, let's try to forget it for today, if we can. Guess there's nothing we can do about it," Alayna said. "Get the cards out and we'll see who is lucky today. Anything to get my mind off this. I'm going to try to have fun!"

The four of us were walking down State Street on another day, on our way to the Student Union on beautiful Lake Mendota. Bubbles and Nick had started dating, and the four of us often did things together. Sometimes we included Margo, but she said

she was busy today. "I hope she is studying," I said. "It seems like she is doing better to me."

"We all have to include her in fun things and get her away from that bad crowd," Ginny said.

"Who would have thought that the four of us would have so much fun together?

I'm pleased that you two are dating," I said. "Should we be planning a double wedding?"

"I wouldn't mind that," Ginny chimed in.

"What are you people talking about? This is going

too far!" said Bubbles.

"We're all adults, so I'll tell you a story that is low-down funny," I said. "Here it is.

A known prostitute who called herself Midnight Dawn came in with a roaring pelvic infection. We took her to the OR and did a D&C, and during the procedure the surgeon found a small marble-sized mass. He brought it to the back table to examine it and found it to be a $100 bill. Since the patient was an addict, she was awake with a block, and he said, "Midnight we found a $100 bill here."

"I'll be damned," she said. "Pete told me he would leave a tip but I never found it! Think I can cash it in?"

The surgeon said, "You can have it after it goes to pathology." "Why, don't they know what a $100 bill looks like?"

"That's hilarious," said Bubbles, even though she was blushing. "I'm not quite used to stories about prostitutes. Teachers are a little bit Pollyanna-like about these things, although sometimes the stories in the teacher's lounge are a tiny bit risqué with certain teachers."

"You can say that again!" Nick says. "Some teachers really get wound up, but maybe it's only the high school teachers. Here's a teacher story.

"Marguerite is a teacher who taught English her entire life. Everyone loved her as a person and as a teacher, fellow teachers and students alike. She always had many plants in her room, near the windows. Teachers always say the plants grow well in classrooms, and they're good for the students.

"One day there was a healthy new plant on the windowsill in the midst of all the other plants. Marguerite said, 'I wonder where that beautiful plant came from? It's not a species that I know.'

"One of the younger teachers whispered to her, 'That is a marijuana plant.

Someone's playing a joke on you!'

"After the students left for the day, Marguerite took the plant away. The next day one of the students said, 'Where is that nice plant that you had on the windowsill?'

"'I don't know where it is. The plant fairy must have taken it away,' Marguerite said."

On this day we were all walking down State Street to the food carts and were eating our food at the Union, watching the boats on the lake.

Bubbles said, "Today there were so many things that went wrong in school. The piano was out of tune and it sounded terrible. The kids were so mean to each other.

They called each other terrible names—hurtful names. Is there a full moon tonight?

"One of my student's name is DeeDee Turner. Another student, Coty, said, 'DDT. Don't touch her. She is toxic! Don't touch her!

"Then DeeDee called Coty, 'Coty Kotex.'

"Another boy said to Anna, 'Anna Isabelle, Anna Isabelle, Anna is a dumb bell!' "I had to send three kids to the office for discipline. I hate to do that.

"Names like Fatso, Four-eyes, Blimp, Tiny, Jumbo, Whopper, Small-fry, the Hulk, Wiseacre, and Smart Aleck are so hurtful, and it's very hard for these kids to ignore and carry on in their classroom studies. Bullies are smart enough not to call others by these names when teachers are around. And so it goes."

"We'll cheer you up, Alayna," said Nick. "We're just the people who can do it.

We'll have our meal and then go to the concert at Shannon Hall, and you'll feel so much better."

"Just being here with you three is good medicine!" Bubbles said.

"Okay, Eric, let's play gin rummy," Ginny says. "I think we have time for one game before the concert."

"Ginny owes me $2580 as of now," I tell them, "and I feel lucky."

"Eric, when we get married and have a joint checking account, I will write you a check for the amount I owe you!"

"I have a one-liner for you" I say. *"A bicycle can't stand alone. It's just too tired."*

"Eric, I think we have you hooked on one-liners. Here's my latest: *A dentist and amanicurist got married. They fought tooth and nail.*

"And you have just passed another test, Erik."

LYDIA'S STORY

I grew up in a little town in Wisconsin named Emerson, on the Mississippi River.

Our family, the Emersons, is a very close-knit family and we all descended from the American poet, Ralph Waldo Emerson. Our town was named after our family, and there is a picture of Ralph Waldo Emerson in the Town Hall.

My early relatives came to Wisconsin three generations ago and started a community with a trading post. The trading post has now become a big general store, which we enlarged through the years. We carry clothing, groceries, hardware, drug items, appliances, hunting guns, fishing gear, jewelry, candy, liquor, toys and various other household items. It's a big store in a little community.

When the railroad came through in 1869, the store became important to the whole area. Animal pelts were traded for food and other objects. The store became a central place for news of the world and trading.

I grew up in a proud German family, and all of us worked in the store as soon as we were old enough. We had a housekeeper because both my parents worked at the store every day except Sunday.

Adaline was one of the family. She lived with us and was our "mother" when Mother was at the store.

Adaline cooked, cleaned, baked and was a constant source of useful information and knowledge for us.

We all learned how to get along with people, even the ones we did not like. We'd whisper to each other about some of the customers as they came in. Gummy Gus, Filthy Fred, Droopy Dick, Darling Dora, Pretty Penny, Gorgeous George, Sleazy Sam, Shy Guy, Luscious Lois, Pale Paul, and others. Everyone had a nickname for us, but we didn't dare call them names in front of our parents.

Our mother was very involved in our Lutheran Church. She belonged to the Ruth Circle (the best circle in the Lady's Aid). They worked hard knitting and crocheting for the poor people, and baking for bake sales and church dinners.

Our German Lutheran church was our family's social life, with Sunday School, pot-luck dinners, Luther League, rummage sales and summer bible camp. We all started singing in the "baby choir", then the junior choir and finally the senior choir. In school we all played a musical instrument. We all went swimming in the summer and ice-skating in the winter. There was a lot of sliding on the hills, and games like Kick the Can, Pomp Pomp Pull-a-Way, King of the Mountain, and many tag games.

My Aunt Hildegard had Larkin Club parties in her home, where she made a lot of food and everyone came to order merchandise from the Larkin Club. The catalog had spices, medicinal items, baking supplies, beauty supplies, bedding, towels, shelves, pots and pans, dishes, silverware and many more items.

My favorite was the raspberry nectar that was sold in concentrated form in glass bottles. We kids called it "Razzleberry" because it was so good—especially in summer when it was so hot. Farmers bought it for haying and threshing times when there were many farmers working together in the summer. The Larkin Club was a social club where everyone was welcome. the more the merrier.

Aunt Hildegard loved it when there was a big crowd of women at the parties, because she got points for selling merchandise. She used the points to get furniture pieces. She got a round oak table and chairs, oak buffet, desk, living room furniture and many small items throughout the years.

This was in competition with my parent's store, but they didn't mind. My mother always went to the parties at Aunt Hildegard's because she would not miss this social party. Everyone came. In fact, Mother ordered cases of Raspberry Nectar to sell in the store. This added to Aunt Hildegard's points, so everyone was happy.

Another favorite item that every house had in their cupboard was Green Drops. The Watkins man came and sold household items to all the houses, and Green Drops was a favorite. If you had a headache, stomachache, backache or leg ache, Green Drops always cured it. Green Drops came in a little square bottle with an eye dropper and all you had to do was put 3 drops in a cup of warm water. It was a miracle. It was a nice peppermint treat for us.

My brother Karl Fredrick started a business; a saloon and boarding house, in a building he built in Emerson.The whole family helped him to get the business going, His wife Louisa, and daughters Gusti, Irna, Gita, and Anna had to work hard to get the business started for Karl's "adventure." They painted, trimmed, decorated, and cooked and cleaned, and it looked like it would work. There were quite a few railroad workers who needed a place to sleep and have fun.

Unfortunately, Karl Fredrick loved to play Sheepshead (Schasfskopf) and drink Schnapps and beer with the other men, became friends with many of them and didn't charge them for the services. His wife and daughters, in the meantime, had to work hard to keep the place going.

Of their children, Gusti and Irna were the first ones to leave and get married.

They married railroad workers who were brothers, and away they went. It wasn't long before Anna and Gita got married and left the village.

Then came the Revolt of Mother. Luisa told Karl that he had to sell the business and get a job or she would leave him. In those days, it was very unusual for the woman to leave her husband, and it would cause a scandal for the family. She told Karl Fredrick that she had heard people talking about them, and used the word "schadenfreude," which means delight in another's misfortune. This was the last straw for Louisa.

They were so lucky that a blacksmith and his family bought the building and used the downstairs for the blacksmith and the upstairs for a boarding house with bed and meals. Karl Fredrick got a job with the family delivering groceries at the store. That was that!

Wisconsin farmers rented a threshing machine every year to separate grain from the seeds at the end of the summer. Farmers went from farm to farm helping in the threshing, as it took many farmers to do the job. It was always hot during the threshing time, and the men worked hard to get it done.

The wives of the farmers baked pies, cakes, bread, and cooked huge amounts of food to feed the farmers. It seemed like each farm wife outdid the other, and the food was absolutely fabulous. Makeshift tables were put together out of long boards set on sawhorses, with benches to sit on. After working so hard in the hot sun, the farmers loved having a big meal and socializing with their neighbors outside.

My grandparents always had Raspberry Nectar in a big earthenware crock with a ladle and glasses handy. Gramma also had hot coffee, milk and water. The men needed lots of liquids after working. We kids carried jugs of water to the men during the day.

Our family had a very large apple orchard with many different species of apples. In the fall, our family picked apples together and made apple butter, apple pies and my favorite—chunky, spicy apple sauce, which we kids all called apple sassy. Um Um Good!

Our high school was so much fun. I was a cheerleader and we went to all the games. We also participated in forensics, debate and clubs. After high school, I went to the School of Nursing at UW in Madison and became a surgical nurse at UW Hospital. I loved Madison and I still do My nurse friends from UW are still my most valued friends.

I met Sean in surgery, where he was the surgeon and I was a surgical nurse. It was a long time before Sean asked me for a date, but after that one date we hit it off and knew this was it! I'm so happy that we found each other.

Sean and I have three amazing children. Our oldest,

Erik, is a surgeon at UW Hospital, as is his father and grandfather, Hans. Hans is semi-retired. It's unusual for three generations of surgeons to be at the same hospital, and our family is proud of them.

Erik is getting married to Ginny this summer. He had been engaged to Julia and we all loved her, but as we get to know Ginny, I think Erik will be very happy with her In his life. I love the fact that Ginny and I both went to the School of Nursing. She is a lovely girl.

We had Ginny to dinner, and we had fun talking about cases we knew about at UW Hospital. Ginny has a delightful sense of humor and is a great storyteller. It means a lot to me to see my children happy, and I can tell that Erik is happy with Ginny.

Nick, our middle child, is a chemistry teacher at East High School. Sean had encouraged Nick to go into the medical field like most of our family, but he was not interested. He has always wanted to be a teacher, and his students are lucky to have him as their teacher. I am happy that Nick had the courage to do what he wanted to do. I'm sure he had guilt feelings about not going into the medical field, and I'm sorry about that.

Margo is our daughter and she is a delightful girl, if I do say so myself! She is in the School of Nursing, and I hope and pray that she makes it. She loves to party and it seems like she is not a serious student. I'm worried that she is in the wrong group of friends. Nursing is difficult and I know she is having trouble with anatomy.

I wish she would settle down and stop running around all the time. She seems oblivious to our suggestions that she must work harder to get her degree. We all offer to help her with Anatomy; we all have a background in medicine. She says NO.

As Sean's wife there are many social activities connected to the hospital. We belong to the Nacoma Country Club, where we all golf and play tennis. There are dinners and dances there that we attend. Our church also has many social functions that we all love. We also love to go to Emerson to visit our family. My parents are getting up in age, and I love to go and help when I can.

Sean had an opportunity to practice at Johns Hopkins Hospital. It was an important compliment just to be invited to join their staff. I really did not want to move away from our family, church and city. I love Madison! After all, money and prestige are not everything. I hope that Sean does not object to my opinion. In the end, it's his decision.

I volunteer at Attic Angels Retirement Home, which has a very good reputation in the Madison area. The training is strenuous, and we pay dues to volunteer, with a

$100 fee to join. We spend time with the residents, take them shopping, and take them to appointments. It is a wonderful group of volunteers, and we do good things in the community.

I thank God that I have Sean and our children.

Sean and I invited the Martini family to dinner. There was delicious food, and everyone was in a good mood and telling stories.

Nick says, "You have all told great stories about surgeries and the health field, and now I will tell you some stories about school events.

"One of my teacher friends teaches 4th grade. She and some chaperons went on a field trip to the

Milwaukee Zoo with a busload of exuberant children. It was a nice, warm day and everyone was so excited about the trip.

"Each child had a buddy and was told to stick close to the group. At the end of the day we all boarded the bus, but Glen said he couldn't find his buddy, Johnny. Glen said, 'I have looked and looked for Johnny and I can't find him!'

"All of the adults went in all directions, and finally the teacher found him wandering around. She took his hand and noticed that his pants were all wet. Maybe he had an accident and was embarrassed, she thought.

"She took Johnny's hand and had him sit with her on the bus. After a while, he said, 'Can you keep a secret?'

'Yes,' she said, 'but only if it doesn't hurt anyone.'

'Look in my backpack. I have something very special in it.'

"The teacher looked in the backpack and immediately shouted, 'Stop the bus!' "We all gathered around and saw a tiny baby penguin in the backpack. Johnny

said, 'I thought you would keep my secret! I always wanted a pet of my own. I even named him Sammy!'

"The teacher told him, 'Johnny, Sammy needs his mother to take care of him.

Animals take care of their babies in a special way, and Sammy needs this special care. I know that you want Sammy to grow up and have fun with his mother and other penguins.'

'I guess you're right, but I am so disappointed. Can I hold him until we get back to the zoo?' Johnny said.

'Of course you can. I'll wrap Sammy in my nice soft scarf and you can hold him.'

"The bus driver called the zoo and told the story. We turned around and headed back. When we got there, three or four zoo keepers took the baby penguin and examined it. Everything looked all right. They asked us not to advertise the event because there could be a copy-cat occurrence."

"How did Johnny get under the fence? Why didn't anyone see him?" Bubbles wondered. Then she said, "Now it's my turn to tell a few stories of things that have happened at school.

"Christmas programs are a big thing in school. I had planned a kind of sing-a- long program with Rudolph and the reindeers leading the singing. I had chosen a bright and outgoing boy to be Rudolph, and he was doing a great job until he started to jazz it up, and walked fast with the rest of the reindeer following him.

"There was a tree in the middle of the stage, and it fell down along with other props for the next act. There was much laughter from the audience and the more they laughed the faster the children ran, all around the stage. Bedlam reigned. I finally got the children to stop running and pulled the curtain on the stage. Parents thought it was the best part of the whole show!

"My friend Melissa was out on the playground with her students one day, and little Mary came running up to her, all out of breath. 'Teacher, Carl said the F word. He said damn it!' Guess it's time to spend more time on phonics."

"Grade schoolteachers are very kind and loving. The students in this age group need attention and love. The grade schoolteachers I know all had boxes of mittens, hats, gloves, boots, tops and pants in their classrooms. Kids came to school many times without warm clothing, or dirty clothing, which made the kid an outsider.

"Teachers often bought soap and washcloths to help the child clean up and feel good about him/herself. Food was another thing that most classrooms had for the little ones who had no breakfast. Now, schools have breakfast for the students, and it is a great thing. Children cannot learn if they are hungry.

"Bullying is another problem in most schools. Teachers have to watch out for the bullies. It's a problem that has existed for generations, and I don't know the answer to the problem, but it is so hurtful. Many kids cannot deal with it, and their grades fall along with their self-esteem

"Charlie, in fourth grade, had diabetes and his teacher had the foresight to invite the school nurse to tell the class about diabetes. After the talk, one little girl asked if Charlie could give her diabetes if she took a drink from the fountain after Charlie. I thought, Oh my, I'm glad the nurse cleared that up. Imagine how the class would stay away from Charlie if they thought that!

"Some teachers help students after school with math or reading. They also give them clothing and hair clips and extra work sheets that they can do at home. It's good to do these things without the other students looking on."

Then Gino told everyone about his last trip to Mexico to buy stock for the store. "Those people down there are so talented, and so much fun to be with. They are trying to teach me some of their songs and are trying to teach me how to play the guitar. I think that if I were down there for a time I would learn to play."

"Dad, you could learn to play here and go down and surprise them! I know a good guitar teacher," Ginny said.

"Wow, do you think this old man could learn? I would love that, but it takes lot of practice. Do I have time?" Gino said.

"Next time we come to your house, I want to hear you play the guitar, Gino. Take time to do the things you want to do," said Sean. "Life is short!"

SEAN'S STORY

I am Sean Schwantes, husband of the lovely Lydia and father of three great children. I am a surgeon with an interesting life, and my father, Hans, was also a surgeon. I am so proud to say that my oldest son, Erik, is a surgeon too, and there are three generations of surgeons at UW Hospital.

I encouraged my other son, Nick, to also go into the medical field, but he was not interested. He has always wanted to be a teacher, and I'm happy that he is strong enough to do what he is destined to do. I was wrong to make an issue of it. I know that Nick was unhappy about it. I must make it up to him and let him know how proud I am of him.

We have a vivacious and pretty daughter, Margo, who is in nursing school at the UW. She has always done so well in school, but I think she is not doing so well now. I am worried about her. She seems to think UW is for having fun, and I hope she gets it out of her system soon. Lydia is a nurse and a good role model for Margo, but I know she is worried about her too.

Our lives revolve around Bethel Lutheran Church, which we dearly love, UW Hospital, and Nakoma Country Club. We all play golf at the club and we love the dinners and dances there. There are many medical activities we participate in and in my opinion we have an interesting and well balanced life.

I had an opportunity to go to the Johns Hopkins Hospital a while ago, and I was disappointed that Lydia did not want to move. Now that I think more of it, much as I hate to admit it, she was right. Our children are here and we go to Lydia's family in Emerson to check on her aging parents often. It's good our children have grandparents and family. We all love to go there.

Now the wedding is being planned, and everyone is caught up in the festivities.

We all love Ginny, her sisters, brother and her mother, but her father is a bit unorthodox. I don't think he approves of Eric for his daughter. I hope that I am wrong, but he does not seem happy about the wedding.

The rehearsal dinner will be at the club, the wedding will be at St. Joseph's Catholic Church, and the reception at the Martini home. I'm so happy that our Rev. Nelson can be a part of the ceremony. I am told that the Martini family is very busy getting ready for the reception and building an in-ground swimming pool. Sounds like fun.

I can't get over the fact that Gino won his house in a poker game. It's really a beautiful house and I must get the story about it. Ginny says she did not want to move, and she loved their house on Regent Street.

The other day I was in the staff OR lounge and someone suggested we go to the local watering hole to catch up on what happened during the day in surgery.

"Let's walk, it's only a few blocks," somebody said.

"No, no no. I'm tired. Let's take the cars," was the response.

"You wimps! Let's get walking," and we set off.

"You're right, it was a nice walk and I feel energized all over," said with sarcasm dripping.

"You're full of it, George. Now, what happened in surgery that was interesting today?"

"Well, I had a logger who came in and he had cut off his finger with his chain saw. I asked him if he had the finger, so I could try to reattach it to his hand.

"He said, 'Well, I wanted to do that, but my finger fell on the ground and my dog, Scamp, ate it!.' Some guys have a big black cloud following them!"

George goes on, "I must tell you what happened yesterday at the hospital. My friend Max was performing a parathyroidectomy and would be implanting several very small pieces of the parathyroid, which was challenging. He wanted to consult his CT scans, which were very meticulously arranged in order.

"He asked the circulating nurse to take the first scans down and add a new CT film to the view box for him. She got up and took down all his films, and put up a new one. He tried to stop her but was watching in horror as she seemed to be shuffling a deck of cards with his CT films. He soon gave up, and all of us who were scrubbed started chuckling, as he growled, '%&*$%@#, what is she doing?' The RN just sat down, oblivious to the whole event while we were all dying with laughter, the surgeon included."

Doc Bram said, "I had a patient who came in the OR today who had Prader Willie's Disease. She literally would eat anything in her environment, and today she came in after swallowing a Bic pen, which was lodged in her stomach. We retrieved it, and found that after being in her stomach it still wrote just fine! That would be a great commercial."

"What was the score of the Badger game last night?" somebody changed the subject. "I'm betting on the Badgers for basketball this season. Both the men and women's teams are great."

"I love the women's hockey team. Lots of action and razz-ma-tazz."

"One more drink and I'm out of here. We all have early surgeries tomorrow. Wish I could stay in bed just one day a week!"

"Now we have to walk over to our cars at the hospital. Whose idea was it to walk over here?"

"You're all sissies and wimps. You're all weaklings. With that, I will say goodnight. See you all in the morning."

"What fun to come to Bunkys for dinner with our two families," said Carmen. "Good thing we have reservations, because it's so busy."

"I remember coming here for Prom dinners with my friends. The food is always good," Ginny said.

"Now that we have ordered, I want to toast our two families. The more you love each other, the closer you will come to God," says Lydia.

"The three most important phrases a husband can say are; I love you; you are so beautiful; and please forgive me!" says Gino.

"It seems that we have some witty and intelligent people in our families," Eric says. "Nick and Bubbles, I will expect you to tell some school stories, too.

"My ophthalmologist friend told me he had a patient with macular degeneration, who had to put eye drops in frequently," Eric said. "He kept his drops on a shelf in the bathroom along with other bottles. One day he reached for his bottle of drops and took the wrong bottle. He put one drop of glue in each eye! I should call Doc. and see how the patient is."

"Here's one," I said. "A rectal surgeon was performing an anal fistula procedure with the patient's legs in stirrups. He was seated between the patient's legs with the anal speculum inserted. The procedure was well underway when he asked for suction. The surgical tech was supposed to help guide the long suction tube into the anal speculum. She missed and could not make the sharp angled turn and instead inserted the suction tube into the surgeon's ear canal.

"The tech was appalled, as the surgeon yelled, "Wrong hole, my God, was that suction used?" Yes, it was indeed used, and not at all clean. At those times I was always glad the patient was asleep."

Nick had a story too. He said, "My friend was a student at a college in upper Michigan and he wanted to become a woodworking shop teacher. His instructor was teaching about safety with woodworking saws, and he said, "Do not ever put your hand under a table saw while it is turned on. Part of the saw is on top of the table and part is under the table." He proceeded to demonstrate what not to do and two of his fingers were cut off! I don't think any of the students will forget this lesson."

"Another pleasant evening with the Martinis and Schwantes families. We are so lucky to have so much fun, and such interesting stories," Carmen said. Can you all come over to our house for Gino's birthday next Saturday night?"

"No gifts, please," says Gino.

"We'd be happy to come. I hope our whole family

can come," says Lydia.

"Yes, of course," Carmen said. "Please extend the invitation to all of you. I hope that Margo can come, too. I miss seeing her."

The next Saturday we all went to the Martini home.

"Welcome to our home for Gino's birthday party," Carmen said. "Drinks are on the patio, and I'll take your coats. I'm so glad you could all come. Margo, you look fabulous! Michael, take Margo to the patio and show her around. Go out and start a game of croquet with the others."

"Mom always has to organize the activities. I guess it's fun, though," Michael says. "Do you want to play croquet, Margo?"

"Sure, why not? It'll be fun. Are you all finished with your classes now, Michael?" "I have two papers to write, and then—Hallelujah—I'm all finished," Michael

says. "Margo, I have news. I have been accepted at the New York School of Ballet. don't say anything to anyone, because I have not told the others. I'll make the announcement to my family soon. My father will not like it, but he'll have to accept it. It is my dream come true!"

"Michael, I am so proud of you," Margo says. "I have yet to see you in a performance, but I know you are good. I'll come to New York to see you dance."

"It'll take some time, I know, before I'll be dancing in a performance. But, I'll let you know when. It would be great if you could come and see me dance. Maybe a bunch of you could come and we'll celebrate!"

Lydia says, I love your Italian cooking, Carmen. Show me how to cook these dishes."

"Oh, Lydia, I'd love to. There's nothing to it. Sometime you and I can get together and cook a meal. I'd love that!"

After the meal, Carmen calls everyone together. "Time for birthday cards," she announces. "There are so many of them."

Gino steps up and opens the cards. They are so funny. "Thank you all for coming to my birthday party. I love the cards, I think! Some are really funny."

Carmen comes forward with a big, huge bag all decorated in bows. "This is for you, Honey," she says. "It's from all of your family."

"What in the world? It's a guitar."

"We all want you to take lessons and play for us here, and when you go down to Mexico, surprise your Mexican friends," says Carmen.

"I am so surprised. I have always wanted to learn to play. Michael, maybe you can help me find a good teacher. Michael is good in music. I am so proud of him," Gino says.

Michael says, "I guess this is a good time to make my announcement. I have been accepted at the New York School of Ballet, and I will be leaving next week. I am so happy to be accepted, as I have always wanted this. The weeks I spent in Ballet School in New York last summer were the best weeks of my life, and now I will be able to do this full time. I can't believe my good luck."

"It wasn't good luck, Michael," said Carmen. "It was years and years of work building your stamina and muscles and practicing dance. You have done so well in everything. I think we have turned the corner in the twists and turns of our lives in this family,"

"We are all so happy for you." "Congratulations."

"Much happiness in New York City." "I couldn't be happier for you." "What an honor."

"It couldn't happen to a nicer guy."

And from Gino, "I can't wait to see you on Broadway!"

MARGO'S STORY

I am Margo, daughter of Lydia and Sean Schwantes, and I have two brothers, Erik and Nick. We live in Middleton, on the West Side of Madison, Wisconsin, on Lake Mendota. I love our neighborhood and family.

We belong to the Nakomas Country Club and we all play golf. Our social life revolves around the club, with dinners, lunches and golf and tennis. I went to Madison Preparatory School (MPS), which is prestigious and difficult. We all had to work hard to excel in our studies, which was expected of us all. After all, it was expensive to go there and we must all work hard, our parents said. My brothers and I all felt the pressure of going there.

My best friend, Marcelle is smart, and she, like me, works hard. My parents say she is a good influence on me. Marcelle's mother is a great and talented seamstress and she makes all of Marcelle's clothing, but I have heard some of the snobs here say that they do not have the "right" labels on them! I carefully cut out labels from my clothes, gave them to Marcelle and told her to sew them on her clothes. This is terrible how mean some of the girls are.

I am so proud of my father and mother. Dad is a surgeon at UW Hospital, and Mother was a nurse until we kids came along. My brother, Erik is a surgeon at

UW too, and my brother, Nick is a chemistry teacher. I have to study hard to make my family proud of me. I'm afraid I have not done that at UW.

Our family loves sports and we go to all the UW football, basketball and tennis matches. We love swimming, ice-skating and events at the Overture Center—plays and concerts.

My mother's family lives in a small town in Wisconsin on the banks of the Mississippi River, named Emerson. We have so many relatives there with so many fun things to do. I often wish that we had lived there with all our relatives. Oma and Opa (my grandparents) are the perfect grandparents. I love them so much.

Now I am at the UW School of nursing, and it is so hard. I know that if I worked hard like I did in high school I would do well, but I am having so much fun. I have a lot of friends who do not work hard, and it seems to have rubbed off on me.

I hope that my family does not know that I smoke pot, because they would be sad, and I would hate that. Everyone I know smokes pot and I have been encouraged to try the hard stuff, but I am afraid of that. I have seen what it can do to a person.

What am I doing to my future? Maybe I should buckle down and work. Maybe I should call Marcelle and renew our friendship. She is a Physics major at UW.

Erik and I have always been close, and I am excited about the coming wedding in our family. Erik was engaged to Julia, but I guess it didn't work out. We all liked Julia, but I think I like Ginny better. She's so much fun, and I think I will finally have a sister.

I'm so happy that I will be in the wedding party.

My brother, Nick is more serious than Erik but I love him dearly. He has always helped me when I needed help in school and out of school. Dad wanted Nick to be a doctor, but Nick always wanted to be a teacher, and he is a great teacher. His students are lucky.

I can't wait for the wedding. Ginny's sister, Olive is sewing all the dresses—can you imagine that? What a talent. I think the emerald green will be outstanding. I think the girl's names are a stitch: Ginny Martini, Olive Martini, Bubbles Martini and Sherry Martini.

I really like Michael, Ginny's brother. He is drop-dead handsome, and he doesn't know it. We are both at the UW, and I hope that we can do something together, although he is graduating this year. He is shy, and I'll have to invite him to something he likes to do. I know he loves music and dance, so maybe I can get some tickets to a musical at the Overture. This may be my way to change my lifestyle.

I am delighted that I will be in the wedding party. Thank you, Ginny for inviting me to be a part of the wedding.

NICK'S STORY

I am the middle child of Sean and Lydia Schwantes, and we live in a big old house in Middleton with neighbors who are fun and good friends. We all play golf and tennis at the Nakoma Country Club and follow all the sports in Madison.

My brother, Erik, my sister Margo and I all went to Madison Preparatory School from K through high school. Then I earned a BS degree from UW in the School of Education, and I now teach science at East High School.

I love teaching. My father wanted me to become a doctor like many in my family, but I have always wanted to teach. I have been teaching for three years, and I am still learning how to be a good teacher. Thank God for my mentor, Allison. She's been teaching for 20 years. I hope my father will be proud of me some day.

Our family has driven up north for vacations for years. We always go to the Holiday Acres Resort on beautiful Lake Thompson, near Rhinelander. Wisconsin. The first year we went there, we only had a week. After that, we rented a cabin for two weeks. It is the best vacation we could ever have.

There are boats of all kinds at the resort—pontoon boats, paddle boats, rowboats and water skiing boats. We swim, fish, ride horses, eat in their great restaurant, or play board games with the kids at the resort.

Owners of the resort are the Zambons. Their kids, Jamie (Margo fell in love with him), Kate (I fell in love with her), and Pete. Pete is like our little brother. I always thought it would be fun to go to school in Rhinelander with our friends, the Zambons.

Now Alayna (Bubbles) and I are dating, and it looks like she has told Patrick that they are over. Alayna is the first girl that I have wanted to take home to meet our family. I think that this is it.

I really like Bubbles. She's beautiful and so much fun, and she's a teacher who loves teaching, just like me. I have to say that Bubbles Martini is quite a name.

Someone in that family has a sense of humor!

I am so worried about my sister, Margo. I don't see much of her these days, even though we live in the same house. I'm afraid that she's running around with the wrong kids. I hope she isn't doing drugs. What should I do about it?

We are at Ginny's great-grandmother GG's favorite restaurant, Tutto Pasta Trattoria, on State Street. She loves the outside table so she can see all the people passing. She's a people watcher.

"GG, tell us a story. You always have a good one to tell," Ginny says.

"One day I rushed to my favorite store after work, just before four," GG begins. "They were having a great sale, and I tried on many different items of clothing in the changing room. Lots of them! When I opened the door, I found that the store had closed, and it was very dark out at five o'clock in the winter.

"What do I do? If I opened the door, I knew bells and

whistles would go off and the police would come. Then I remembered the name of one of the salespeople and looked for a telephone. I called him, and as luck would have it, he was home, and he came and unlocked the door for me. I felt like a Dipsy Doodle, but he was very nice to me. Those were the days, when stores closed at five every day and closed on Sundays. I had picked out two outfits to buy, but I didn't have the nerve to ask him to sell them to me."

"Are you ready for a very morbid, gloomy story of James that will turn your stomach and make you nauseous?" said Erik.

"James (not his real name) was devastated because his wife died. He just could not get over it, and he went to her grave to talk to her every day after work. Some nights, he fell asleep lying over her grave and woke up after hours of grief.

"James started to feel sick to his stomach and when it got worse and worse he went to the doctor. All the tests came back negative, but he was getting so sick that he couldn't go to work. He spent long hours at his wife's grave day and night.

"His doctor ordered a CT scan, and it showed foreign matter around in his intestinal area. A surgeon went in for exploratory surgery and was amazed by what he saw. Hundreds and hundreds of black beetles about 1/2 inch long were all around and about the pelvic area. This is virgin territory, and he didn't know what to do. He scooped as many as he could out and closed up. Everybody in the surgical team was horrified by what they saw.

"Nobody knew how this could happen, but they speculated that James slept on the grave with his mouth open, and the beetles crawled in and started a colony. This is a very weird situation that is hard to believe, but it happened.

"After the surgery, the doctor prescribed the same treatment that is used for a colonoscopy to purge and clean the body and hopefully get rid of all the creepy-crawly critters. I never heard if this worked."

I said, "I don't do a good job telling stories, so just bear with me. Here are some high school stories.

"Seniors in high school think they can do anything on the last day of school. One of those last days a student brought a greased pig and let it run in the school. Pandemonium followed, with students and teachers trying to catch the pig. After a time, a teacher called the police and they came with a big net and caught the pig. It was funny, but nobody knew who brought the pig!

"One year two seniors rode bikes up and down the halls of the high school. They were not very smart, because their diplomas were held back."

"I think you do an incredible job of telling a story, Nick Those are all so fantastic and entertaining," said Carmen. "I am so happy that our two families are getting together. I am having so much fun! Please tell us more of your stories the next time we see you."

"Tell us another story, GG," Ginny said. "I love your funny stories."

"The trouble is, they are all true," GG said. "How could I possibly do the things I do?"

"One day GG Tony mowed the lawn and put the lawn mower away in the garage. We always backed the car into the garage, and we had an electric mower. Somehow, the electric wire from the lawn mower got tangled up on the bumper on the car, and when I drove the car out of the garage, the lawn mower was bumping along the behind the car. Everyone waved at me and I waved back and thought, my, how friendly everyone is today.

Where is that loud noise coming from? It sounds like something is wrong behind the car, I wondered to myself. Then I stopped at the Stop sign, and a nice old man told me my lawn mower was bouncing on the road behind me. I couldn't believe it.

Someone was taking pictures of the mower and the car, and people were laughing, I think I made their day!"

CARMEN TELLS THE WEDDING STORY

Preparations for the wedding go on in a frantic and stressful manner on this, the Friday before the wedding; food for the reception is ordered; flowers will be delivered; decorative tents or canopies are ordered for the morning; the wedding cake will be delivered at noon; tables, chairs and dishes will be delivered by noon; lace table cloths will be delivered in the morning, and now we can go and enjoy ourselves at the rehearsal dinner.

The in-ground pool is really stunning, with an attractive setting all around the pool, and Gino is so proud of it. "Don't you think this will be a perfect setting for the reception?" he asks me.

"It really is so much nicer than I thought it would be!" I reply. "I guess you were right again, Gino. I hate to say it," I laughed. "Now let's get changed to go to the rehearsal dinner."

Our whole family drove to the Nacoma Country Club and we were all in a fun and agreeable mood. The country club was ablaze with lights and flowers. As soon as we arrived, I noticed that Gino was ill-at-ease. I whispered to the girls to spend time and give extra attention to their father. I think it worked!

Andre, the ring-bearer and Jordan, the flower-girl stole the show. They are cousins of Erik and they are really sweet. Sean and Lydia went out of their way to make us feel welcome, and the children were fun to be with.

The food was so delightful and served with good taste. The two entrees were filet mignon and fish baked in champagne, and both were delectable.

Our two families exchanged stories about Erik and Ginny that were entertaining and funny. Nick and Bubbles seemed to have a great time talking and exchanging stories about their teaching careers. They seemed to know other teachers in Madison and had a great deal in common.

We toasted the young couple with champagne. Gino toasted, "May good luck be your friend in whatever you do, and may trouble be always a stranger to you."

Sean toasted, "First take care of business, then drink and laugh!"

Father Danny prayed before and after the dinner. He is such a great friend of our family. Rev. Nelson was there with good words of advice for our young people.

The evening ended with good cheer and happiness for Erik and Ginny. They looked so happy, and I have to say that Ginny was ravishing for all to see.

Today's the day! The sun is up, and it's going to be a marvelous day.

Ginny tries on her dress, and it's a dream come true. Her hair is beautiful, her makeup perfect, and all is well with the world. I want to take pictures of Ginny and her father in front of the pool, so Gino makes a big deal out of escorting his lovely daughter to the pool area.

I got two or three good pictures, and then a terrible thing happens. Somehow, Ginny falls into the pool. Does Gino push her in? No, I thought. He couldn't do that to her.

But Gino says, "Now you cannot marry Erik. It's all for the best." Ginny and I are both crying and punching Gino as he says he is innocent.

Olive sees what has happened, and she says, "I wanted to make your dress, Ginny, and now I am going to!" She takes the sobbing Ginny into the house and tells her to wash her face and do her makeup again. Olive takes charge and tells Bubbles to get the hairdryer and fix Ginny's hair. "We'll have you beautiful in an hour," she says.

"Bubbles get my long white, strappy nightgown and put it on Ginny. Then get two of the big lace tablecloths off the tables and bring them here," Olive says. " Also, get my big sewing kit from my bedroom We don't have a minute to waste."

Olive starts sewing, but it's too slow. "Bubbles get the stapler from the workshop. This is going to take some imagination," she says. She staples the lace together and adds flowers to hide the staples. Ginny cannot stop crying.

Meanwhile, back at the church Andre, the little ring bearer decides that he does not want to walk down the aisle in that big church with all the people in it. Jordan, the little flower-girl, tries to talk him into it, but he says, "No!"

Sherry looks all around the church and finds a

little boy the same size as Andre. She asks his parents if Grayson can be the ring-bearer and explains the situation. The parents, relatives of the Schwantes, say yes. Grayson is excited about it. "I've never been in a wedding before," he says. Grayson puts on Andre's clothes and Andre puts on Grayson's clothes, and they fit. The tuxedo is perfect on Grayson.

Problem solved.

The guests are all seated and the music is terrific. The ring-bearer and the flower-girl come down the church aisle looking enchanting. Then the bridesmaids come. The emerald green dresses are exquisite. Olive, Sherry, Bubbles and Margo look absolutely gorgeous, and Jordan looks like an angel in her emerald green dress. "I love

this wedding. I get to toss flowers all over the floor of the church. This is fun!" she says.

Finally the bride and father walk towards the altar. The bride looks sort of flustered, and her dress is whimsical. Sean and Lydia whisper that Ginny's wedding gown is different. What happened to it, and where did this gown come from? Lydia wonders.

They get to the altar, and Gino decides that he does not want to "give" his daughter to Erik. This could be a bad scene. Everyone is wondering what is going on. Gino is pulling Ginny away, and so I march up, take him by the arm and march him to the front seat. That was that!

Ginny is flabbergasted by her father's show of defiance, but further amazed when she sees Father Salvatori at the altar. Where is Father Danny? Ginny's sisters and I all panic when we realize that Father Danny is not there. His brother has died, and he had to do the funeral, it turns out later.

The wedding must go on. Ginny hisses at Father Salvatori, "You molested me." When it comes time to go to communion, Ginny, her sisters and I all go to Rev.

Nelson, along with all the Schwantes'. The Martini relatives are all wondering what is going on.

After the ceremony, Gino asks me what is going on. I finally tell him all about Father Salvatori. Gino furiously goes to find Father Salvatori.

"Father Salvatori, you God-damn hypocrite! I'm going to do two things to you," Gino declares. "One, I'm going to chop it off, and two, I'm going to the bishop tomorrow to tell him that we have a monster in our church who is doing evil and disgusting things to our children. I'd like to kill you."

"You are the first to know that I am leaving the Catholic Church right now," Father says. "The church is wrong to not let priests marry and have families, and I am going to marry Sister Ann and live as a family. The little child that the nuns have been taking care of is mine. I can at last take care of Ann and little Jeremy.

"I have a position in the Episcopal Church, and we can start a new life. Thank God for that."

"Don't thank God for anything you repulsive devil. And do not come to the wedding reception at my home this afternoon. I never want to see you again. I can't believe that I invited you to my daughter's reception."

The lawn is delightfully stunning with flowers everywhere and a champagne fountain in the middle of the table arrangement. Gino has seemed to accept his role in the reception and is circulating among the guests.

The pool is a big success with many of the kids splashing around in it. Gino is so proud of the pool and the whole setting for the reception. He is still horribly angry at Father Salvatori, but he has decided that he will not spoil Ginny's wedding reception.

There are many different eccentric and unique guests here. One of them is Ralph, who is a nurse at UW Hospital. He rides in on his bicycle and gets into a conversation about how he has not ridden in a car for years, because he does not want to polute the air. He walks, bikes and in bad weather takes the bus where ever he goes.

He hides his very expensive Trek mountain bike behind the house and then starts discussions about cars versus bicycles. Most people seem to know Ralph and go along with his banter and babble.

Another group of people were taking about Governor Walker's cut to education. "Now teachers have to use their own money to buy necessary supplies for their classes," one points out. "The vouchers that Wisconsin pays for are thousands and thousands of dollars that could be used in the public schools. What is the matter with those Wisconsin law-makers who pass such crazy laws!"

"I am so angry that Governor Walker does not allow us to use stem cells from aborted fetuses. He thinks it's better to throw it all out, instead of using it for vital research. He's living in the Dark Ages!"

"I think it would be morally wrong to use aborted fetus stem cells," someone else objects. "I think Walker is right!"

A group of doctors were listening to the conversations with great interest. This has been debated in Wisconsin for many years, and most of them think research with stem cells is greatly needed.

"Governor Walker's tax cuts for the wealthy are fantastically foolish. They help the wealthy and do not "trickle down" like Walker thinks they do. What kind of society do we live in?"

"Oh, come on the middle class is getting tax cuts, too. Where have you been?"

I hear all this and decide to announce that the wedding meal is ready. "Everyone find a seat and we will all enjoy a meal with our newly married couple."

The dinner is announced, and the feast begins. Sherry's former partner, Tasha and her assistants have surpassed the norm with the magnificent food. Presentation is impressive with just the right touches of color, and the arrangement of flowers.

Rev. Nelson prayed before the magnificent dinner was offered. The prayer was sincere and classic, with personal references to Erik and Ginny. This was a perfect way to start the meal. The Martini family seemed to really like Rev. Nelson, and I was amazed when I saw Gino enjoying a talk with him after the dinner. I wondered what they were talking about and what Gino was saying that made him so happy and cheerful. I'll bet Gino has never talked to a Lutheran minister before.

Nick, Erik's best man, had the first toast. "May you always have work for your hands to do. May your pockets hold always a coin or two," he toasted.

Olive, Ginny's maid of honor said, "May your days be many and your troubles few."

Erik's father had the next toast. "A good memory is one that can remember the day's blessings and forget the day's trouble."

Gino is up next with this toast: "Everyone hears the music differently, but the dance together is wonderful."

Throughout the dinner, guests tapped their glasses with calls for; "Kiss the bride!;" "Long live love;" and "Long live the newlyweds."

There was much laughter and good humor, and Ginny finally turned about and threw her wedding bouquet of flowers, right into Bubbles' hands. There was much laughter about that! Bubbles said, "I don't think I'll be the next bride!" Erik and Ginny changed their clothes and got into the car that had been decorated with colorful language and streamers. Away they went.

As soon as the bride and groom left, two men in suits from the IRS came and asked where Gino was (Gino had seen them, and made an exit through the back yard.) I asked them again what they wanted Gino for, and they explained that they just wanted to question him about the house he won in a poker game. They said they had been wanting to question him for a long time, and they just couldn't find him. They would be back.

Gino is thinking, I'll just avoid them and maybe it will go away. I don't think I have a problem. I wonder if my good friend Mark called them?

Ralph gets up and says, "I have to get to work at the hospital." He goes to get his bike, and it is gone! He panics and looks all around. Michael had seen his father ride off on a silver blue bike when the IRS men were looking for him.

Michael says, "Here, take my bike and come back tomorrow for yours. I'm sure it will be here then. Be sure to bring my bike back."

"Are you sure?" I love that bike, but I have to go to work. I'll see you tomorrow.

You're sure it will be here?" Ralph says.

"Yes. I'll be sure to have it here for you." With that, Ralph rode off, very agitated.

The next day, both families got together for the gift opening at the Martini home.

Erik and Ginny were there, and they planned to leave for their honeymoon trip right after the event.

After the gift openings there was a very loud roar, and we all turned around to see what happened. The cement from the swimming pool had collapsed and the pool was full of cement pieces. Thank God there were no kids in the pool.

What a commotion. As Gino was looking down into the pool, the two IRS men came from behind him and took him away for questioning. They were nice about it, but we were all in shock. I told Erik and Ginny to forget that this happened and go on their trip. Erik's family was mortified for our family. Confusion reigned.

THIS HAS BEEN A HELLOVA WEDDING!

The IRS men questioned Gino for a long time. They determined that he had not paid tax on the Middleton house. The appraisal for the house had been 'way too low, and now we owe a considerable amount of money in taxes. If we cooperate and pay the taxes, we will not be prosecuted. We do not have the money. What will we do?

Gino's "good buddy," Mark came over to the house and asked if we could talk. I wonder how he knew that the IRS men had talked to Gino? Could it be that he had called them?

Mark said, "I have been going through hell and back because my wife, Lois is so mad at me. She has threatened to divorce me, and the girls are furious with me. They all want our house back and I'll do anything to get it back. Can we make a deal?"

" I can tell you right now that I will not give the house away," Gino said. "You, of all people, know how much the house is worth."

"Okay, buddy," Mark says. "Can we talk and make a deal in a sensible way?

You've got me over a barrel 'cause my family won't talk to me."

"The IRS people seem to have an accurate appraisal on the house. Do you agree with me?" Gino says.

"I guess you're right. I hate to admit it, but I'm buying my own house back. I'll pay the appraisal price just to make peace in my family. I had to promise that I will never play poker again or gamble again. Something happens to me when I gamble. It's like a disease, because I can't stop even when I know I am going to lose. Guess it's like an addiction," says Mark.

"I know it's hard for you to admit all this." Gino said. "This has been terrible for me, too. The IRS men came to my house right after we had the wedding gift party for our daughter, with all of her in-laws there. It was not a pretty picture."

In the end, we sold the house to Mark, and I found

a nice little house in the Bush, where we belong. We can pay the taxes and have enough money to buy the new house, and now we own Martini Boutique and our little house. We do not have any debts, and GG says that this was all preordained.

"How did I ever get into such a mess?" Gino says. "This was a twist of fate."

I am correct and proper about the whole thing. I say, "All's well that ends well."

GG FRANCESCA'S STORY

I am so sad today. I'm thinking of my children and grandchildren in Palermo. I miss them so much and I always pray for them. There is a hollow place in my heart whenever I think of them. How are they, and what do my grandchildren look like? Are they all well? My parents and sisters send us letters and pictures of the children, but it's just so hard. Then August died in the flu epidemic, and we lost another of our children! This has been very hard for me through the years.

A part of me will never forgive Tony for taking me away from my family, even though we have a nice life here. I just wish I could go and visit them all.

I miss going to the outdoor market every day. It was a time for getting together with the village women and laughing and talking. The children played games with each other and had such a good time. After all these years, you'd think I would get over this, but it never gets any easier. I love it here, you know, but my life over there was good, too. America does not have such markets.

It was always fun to watch men playing chess on the oversized chess sets on the village square. We always stopped to watch on our way to get food for the day, as we listened to our very own opera singer singing for us in the market. There were statues of Pinocchio everywhere—some very small and some very big. Pinocchio is kind of a mascot for everyone in Italy.

The markets were so festive and beautiful, with flowers for sale everywhere. The crusty bread was delicious and smelled so good. It was baked in the communal ovens, along with biscotti, and eaten with olive oil and spices. Many different cheeses were available to eat with the bread, too. The sounds and smells of the market are so memorable. Some parts of Italy raised small horses for food, and it was sold all over Italy. As I remember, it was very tender and tasty.

We had a Committee of Good Taste that decided what colors we could paint our houses. We all wanted our village to look nice, so we went along with the committee.

The church was the center of all activities and there were many festivals, with parades and processions crowding our narrow village streets on saint's days. Food, singing, flowers everywhere, and dancing were so much fun. Everyone came out for these occasions.

The olive groves all around the village were important to all of us. At the end of the growing season, the whole village helped pick the olives and worked to make the olive oil, which was used all year long.

Dry stone masons erected stone walls and terraces on the hills for the olive trees and grape vines. They were skillful and fun to watch. There were lookout towers on the mountains and breakwater walls on the ocean. Lovers dove into the ocean from the high towers. Trains went right through the mountains in tunnels built many years ago.

Italians love their beaches, and we were excited to go there. The promenade of people strolling up and down the beaches was so much fun for young and old.

There were storms and high winds from the ocean sometimes in the year. We learned to stay away from the beach those times. It affected the hiking trails too, so we were careful.

Most people in Palermo visited the cemetery, which is high in the hills every week. People brought flowers and prayed for relatives. There were stories about the person written on a framed square marker at each grave, and tons of flowers. I guess this is why I am sad today.

GG Tony has died. I didn't even know that he was ill. He had lung cancer but had refused treatment for months. He said he wanted to do the things he loved, which were spending time with the family and at the hardware store.

His store was a meeting place for men from the Bush. He had a corner of the store with a big coffee pot and a game table where they could play cards. He dearly loved spending time with his friends at the store. They all talked about politics, sports, family affairs, and many other subjects. Somebody always brought rolls or donuts.

Toward the end, I noticed that Tony took pills and looked pale and tired. He finally told me about the cancer, and I urged him to take the treatments. He, of course said no. By then it was probably too late anyway.

Tony was a heavy smoker all his adult life and it finally caught up with him. He coughed a lot, and when he went to the doctor, he was told he had cancer. He didn't want anyone to know, and he didn't want to have chemo treatments. He just wanted to enjoy himself as much as he could with his family and his beloved hardware store.

Tony got his financial papers in order and when he died his family and I did not have to worry about anything. He planned his funeral with a big party for the whole community at the Italian Workman's Hall with food and drink for all. This was a good ending for what he called himself, a not-so-good person. I believe he was a good person.

When he was near death, we were all around his hospital bed hoping that he would come out of the coma that happened after surgery. The cancer had metastasized to his brain, and the surgeon hoped that she could remove the tumor and then deal with the lung cancer. GG Tony never came out of the coma because the tumor was larger than the surgeon anticipated.

His wish was to donate his body to the UW Medical School, and so before he died we called to alert the school. They asked how much GG Tony weighed, and the nurse said 204 pounds. "Then we cannot accept the body," they said. "He would have to be under 200 pounds."

Doc took the phone and said, "I know you need cadavers, and he will weigh under 200 pounds when you come to pick him up! What is the matter with you? Plan to pick him up when we call."

Then the doctor asked us, "Do you mind if I give GG Tony a diuretic? He'll be under 200 pounds in no time,"

"No, we don't mind," I said. " I can't believe we have to worry about weight even after we die." We all had a comment about that, and it was hilarious. I guess it was comic relief after we were so sad and worried. GG Tony would have done the same.

We had a Memorial Service in our church, and we all went to the big party that GG Tony had arranged, with much food, drink and stories about Tony. I wore the official black, long dress for a month after the funeral. Then I decided that I didn't want to wear it anymore. I'm sure Tony wouldn't have wanted me to. All the other widows in the Bush wore black all the rest of their lives, but this is America!

After the funeral, we all went home to a house without GG Tony. It seemed so dull and different from when he was there. I guess I didn't realize how interesting and fun he was until he was gone. Sometimes it seems like I am on a huge treadmill, and I walk and walk and get nowhere. The world moves under me at a fast pace. Sometimes I forget what I remembered!

That night, when I went to my dresser to get my nightgown out of the drawer, I found an old leather bag with a note in it. The bag had some diamonds, emeralds and rubies in iit and a letter to me. There were still those gemstones in the bag, and now I know what happened in Palermo. After all these years, he finally told me. I realized that he was probably ashamed and embarrassed about it, and I am happy that I finally know what happened after all these years. I hope that his brothers learned their lesson and had good and successful lives.

Dear Francesca,

Now that I am gone, I want to tell you the whole story of why we had to leave Palermo.

My two brothers and I got mixed up in wrong company, and we were involved in a robbery with a gun, that turned into a murder. All of us would have been arrested, but I went "on the lam" and left the country with our family so that the authorities would think that I was guilty.

We had to act fast to get away, and my brothers and I gathered all the food and bought the tickets for the voyage for us all. My brothers had orders not to tell anyone, and to say good-bye for us to our family after we left. We had to change our last name, which I truly hated to do. I was so proud of my family name.

I did not kill that man, and I did not get the loot from the robbery. I don't know who did. My reward for doing all of this was money for the ship and all the food and trunks for the trip, and a bag full of diamonds, rubies and emeralds.

I have sold a diamond or two through the years when I needed money.

Remember the new refrigerator I got you for Christmas? And the house that you and I just loved? And the hardware store that I bought when the owners retired? And the grocery store for Sam? Any time I needed money I would go to Goodman's Jewelry store on State Street in Madison to sell some gems. Goodmans is fair and discrete, and they have always been honest with my dealings with them.

Francesca, all the legal papers are in order for the sale of my beloved hardware store. My good friend and faithful employee Luigi didn't have a down payment to buy the store, so I did the legal work to have him buy the store on a land contract. He will make you a monthly payment, so you have income to live. When you die, he will have to get a loan and pay our five children equal amounts of money to pay off the debt. I want Luigi to have the store because he loves it like I do. I want the store to be the same as when I owned it.

You should be just fine because all our debts are paid, and we own our house. I do not want you to have any money worries. My Insurance papers and Social Security papers and all the other papers for the hardware store are all in a packet in the top drawer of the library table.

I know that you have missed your family and friends in Palermo. So, have I, but now you know why we could not go back, even for a visit.

Francesca, I have loved you my whole adult life and I did not want to hurt you. I think that we have made a good life for ourselves and our family. I am so proud of all of our family, and I'm proud of you. You are the best thing that has happened to me.

I am so sorry that I have disgraced my family in Palermo. Your family there too must have been condemned. For that I am sorry. Please forgive me. I know that you have missed our children and grandchildren all these years. I have too, but I could not do a thing about it.

I didn't ask where the money and gemstones came from, because I guess I just didn't want to know! This was a huge sacrifice for me and all of us. I think we have a good life here in Madison, Wisconsin.

All my love, Tony

ACKNOWLEDGMENTS

I wish to express my appreciation to my good friend Lynne Leuthe, who has edited my book with talent and smart rearranging of ideas and characters. It was a giant jigsaw puzzle which required time and competence.

Nancy Homes also spent time and effort editing this book. I would like to thank her and also Caralyn and Gilbert Splett, Bill and Dottie Weiss, Pat Harrington and Bobbi Seim, Mary Rumsey, Janice Hoff, Christina Hovey, Larry Jensen, Sister Zita, Kathrine LeTourneau, Maria Harrington, Debbie Hillebrand, U.W. School of Dance, Ballet School, Susan Binkley, Shirley Parker, Jeanne Goody and my old friends from DNR, Jan and Jim Miller, whose friendship dates back to 1970. The ideas and experiences of these people helped to form an interesting background for my book. I thank them all.

Catherine Tripalin Murray's *Grandmothers of Greenbush,* is an elegant description of early life in Greenbush. I love her homey words. She is quoted in my chapter on the Greenbush.

Dave Cieslewicz, David Mollenhoff and Lindsay

Woodridge wrote an interesting article of early Greenbush, *Greenbush-Vilas Partnership*, which explains how people of the Bush interacted and helped each other in ordinary life. Greenbush was a fine example of immigrant people settling in America and solving problems of everyday life.

My five amazing children, Marie, Bob, Betty, Patty and Joan have contributed stories of their careers in Health Care and Education that I think are interesting and quite extraordinary. The book is full of stories of our family, covering many years. Harvey Martini also contributed.

Two experienced and caring Educators: Sister Helen P. Mrosla, who wrote *A Very Special Story* and Elizabeth Silance Ballard, who wrote *Little Teddy Stoddard* have written touching stories that have made me cry. Their two stories have good ideas that teachers everywhere can use.

CPSIA information can be obtained
at www.ICGtesting.com
Printed in the USA
LVHW110440271021
701667LV00002B/207